Evan

Billionaire Blind Dates

Book 2

Toni Denise

Chapter One
Evan

"Well, Evan, are you excited?" Luke joked.

"About?" Evan asked, confused.

"It's your turn to do the blind dates," Luke laughed.

Evan swallowed. He wanted a woman to spend his life with, but was he ready for blind dates?

A few months ago, he'd been the one to come up with the idea for all of them to take turns picking blind dates for each other, one at a time. These dates were all to play out at a restaurant where he was a silent partner of "The Blind Date."

This restaurant was different from any other one. You met your date in the dark, and you didn't get to find out who your date was until the end, and only if both people agreed. It was a genius idea that he'd immediately backed and believed would do well. So far, it had.

It was starting to get stuffy in here. He looked around Cade's game room as he pulled on his tie. He was less worried about the dates themselves and more worried about if it didn't work.

"Hello?" Luke waved his hand in Evan's face.

He pushed it away. "What?" Evan snapped.

"I think you don't want to do this," Cade commented. "This was all your idea. You can't back out."

"I wouldn't complain if you did," Jake told him.

Jake had gone first. After a run of bad dates, the worst being Luke's pick, he'd finally found a good date in Lauren, who happened to be Cade's secretary.

"You're just saying that because it went well for you," Luke frowned.

"Why do you care?" Evan turned to Luke.

"Because he has some stupid chick picked out for you already," Ryker tossed in his own thoughts with a wave of his tattooed hand.

Evan ran a hand through his thick dark hair. He had to give it a try. He wouldn't know if it would help him find someone unless he tried, and it had worked out well for Jake. Plus, if his friends' picks were bad, he could use the app to match with someone first based on the test you had to take.

"I'm not backing out." He was going to pull that constricting blue tie off now, though.

"Don't let them push you into shit," Jake told him.

"I'm not," he defended. "Fucking hell, whose turn is it?"

The poker game had come to a halt when Luke had asked that question. They played every Friday night, though their group was getting smaller lately with Owen and Jake in serious relationships.

"Yours!" his friends yelled.

"It's been yours ever since Luke tried, and succeeded, to distract you." Cade rolled his eyes and gestured to the cards on the table. "You might as well fold. You aren't even paying attention."

"Whatever." Evan took a look around the table and realized Cade was right.

He tossed his cards face-down on the table and stood. He ignored the laughter from everyone as he walked off to the bathroom.

Closing the door behind him, Evan leaned forward, towards the mirror, bracing himself with his hands on the counter. He had no reason to be this nervous over a few dates. Hell, it wasn't like he'd been doing a good job for himself in that department anyway.

He sighed and stood straight, looking at himself in the mirror. He needed to get it together. He turned on the cold water and splashed some on his face before grabbing the towel off the rack and wiping his hands and face off.

One more deep breath and he was ready to go back to the game. No doubt he'd lost plenty of chips to Luke just then. He needed to get his head back in the game and take them back.

He pulled the door open only to find Jake on the other side. "What?"

"Needed to piss," he shrugged. "Look, don't let them get to you. Your dates will be fine—well, some might. Luke is an asshole, but that comes from being young and dumb."

"Yeah."

He stepped out of the bathroom and allowed Jake to pass him by. The man smiled all the time now and seemed happier than he ever had before. Not that Jake had ever been much of anything else, but now it was a different kind of happy—the kind that came from knowing your other half was waiting for you at home.

Luke, on the other hand, was an asshole. He was the youngest of the group and was still living the high life that came from being a young, attractive man with entirely too much money.

His friend group—Cade, Evan, Jake, Luke, Owen, and Ryker— were all billionaires from different businesses. It was nice to have money, but dating was a challenge when you were looking for something real. Sometimes women would fool them into believing they were sincere, but in the end, they only cared about money.

"You're back. You want in or are you going to sit the rest of the night out while you contemplate your life choices?" Luke called out.

"Deal me in." He took his seat and tried to focus on the cards being dealt.

"I'm out." Jake took his jacket off the back of the chair he had been in moments before.

Luke made a sound like a cracking whip.

"Have a good night, man," Cade told him.

"Yup," Ryker said, always the quiet one of the bunch.

"Yeah, yeah." Jake waved Luke off before letting himself out.

"He's so whipped. He and Owen both," Luke mused aloud.

"You'll want that one day," Evan told him.

"Bullshit. All of you old men can have the wife, picket fence, and 2.5 kids, I'll stick with the good sex with multiple women—at the same time," he added with a wink.

Ryker laughed. "Your dick's gonna fall off, dude."

"What the fuck ever." Luke waved him off and tossed in more chips. "I raise."

"Call." Ryker stared him down.

Evan took a look at the two cards in front of him and called as well. Cade called, and Ryker dealt the last face-up card on the table.

Evan had a good hand and did his best not to shift in his seat and tip his hand. It wasn't that any real money was being exchanged tonight, but he didn't want to lose, either.

Luke smiled. "Raise." He tossed several chips in again.

"Fold." Ryker tossed his cards down and picked up his beer.

"Call." Evan threw in enough chips to meet Luke's bet.

"Fold." Cade leaned back in his chair and stretched.

Luke grinned and turned his cards over. Two pair with kings high. He leaned forward to rake in the chips.

"Not so fast." Evan turned his own two cards over revealing a flush. He'd won, and he pulled all the chips his way.

Luke gaped. "How?"

"I wasn't busy worried about getting laid," Evan told him as he stacked up his chips.

Cade stood and walked towards the fridge. "Anyone need a beer?"

They all said they did as Ryker shuffled the cards for the next hand. Cade came back with a bottle for each of them and passed the bottle opener around.

"Who's going first for Evan?" Cade asked and took a swig of his beer.

"I am." Luke was so matter of fact, anyone would have thought they had already agreed on it.

"Absolutely not," Evan told him.

"What? You want him to go?" He pointed at Ryker.

Evan looked from Luke to Ryker before laughing. "Anything is better than you. Hopefully, someone picks me a good date, and then I won't get to suffer your punishment."

"That's shit. You're just scared." Luke folded his arms and leaned back, staring Evan down.

"Are we twelve? You're going to try to call me a chicken so I agree to let you go first while defending my manhood?" Evan shook his head. "Hate to break it to you, kid, I'm not that dumb."

"Does anyone have a date in mind?" Luke asked.

Cade shook his head. "I think Jake does."

"Well, he's not here." Luke turned to Ryker and arched a brow, waiting for his answer.

"Of course not," Ryker answered.

"See? That means I have to go first because I'm the only one ready," Luke told him.

Evan took a long pull of his beer while he contemplated the implications of letting Luke go first. His date for Jake was bad—a touchy-feely woman with one thing on her mind. Well, probably two: money and sex.

Disgusted with what he was about to do, Evan just stopped himself from slamming the rest of the beer back. "Fine. You can go first."

"Yes." Luke pumped one arm in excitement.

"God, you're such a kid." Evan shook his head and threw back the rest of his beer.

One more hand was played and Evan once again took the pot from Luke who thought he'd won. Luke whined when everyone agreed to call it a night.

"Come on, I deserve a chance to win my chips back." Luke pressed everyone for another hand.

Ryker came around the table and smacked him on the shoulder. "Get ahold of yourself. It's not even real money."

"I don't like to lose," Luke gritted out.

"Then stop doing it," Ryker told him.

Luke pulled his shoulder out of Ryker's grasp. "Shut up."

"It was sound advice," Cade teased.

Luke threw a look at Cade, and he looked so ridiculous that Evan couldn't hold back his laughter.

"Fuck all of you," Luke called out. He headed for the door and yanked it open before slamming it behind him.

The three men left were still laughing as they finished cleaning up.

"One day he will wake up and realize there's more to life than bimbos," Cade assured everyone.

"His dick is gonna fall off," Ryker said, again.

Lately that was the only thing that Ryker ever said about Luke. Luke annoyed the shit out of Ryker, but for some unknown reason, he had decided that Ryker was his mentor but did the opposite of every piece of advice Ryker had ever given him. It was a weird dynamic.

"You better go get your rest. Luke will have that date set up in no time for you, and if she's anything like the one he picked for Jake, you're going to need to be well rested." Cade tossed the empty bottles into the trash.

"Neither of you could have come up with a date? You both backed out on me." Evan stared down his friends.

"Oh no, I've done my part already," Cade said.

"You didn't do shit. Everyone knows Catherine picked for you," Evan told him.

"I let her." Cade put both hands up as though he'd done his part by letting Catherine pick.

"Maybe we should add her to the party. She already knows about it. Then you'll have to actually make your own pick." Evan laughed at Ryker's shocked face.

It was no secret that Catherine had a thing for Ryker. What he didn't understand was why Ryker had never admitted to anyone that he wanted Catherine, too. It was obvious to anyone in a room with both of them for more than five minutes.

"If you think she won't take two turns, then you don't know my sister at all." Cade brushed off the table and walked back to the fridge. "Either of you staying the night?" he asked.

"Not me. I've got shit to do this weekend. I'm out," Ryker said before heading to the door and letting himself out.

"I think my life is about to get real interesting, so I'm going to head home tonight and enjoy the last bit of peace I can before Luke sets me up on a date with someone who will probably turn out to be a fucking escort or some shit," Evan told him, walking towards the door.

"Might not want to say that anywhere near Luke. He'd probably do it and consider it a good business investment because Ryker told him not to," Cade teased.

"Don't say a fucking word," Evan threatened and opened the door.

"Have a good night," Cade called out.

"Yeah, you too," Evan replied.

He headed home to get ready for the weekend and to contemplate the person that Luke might pick out for him. It seemed a lot was about to happen in his life, but only time would tell if it would be good news or not.

Chapter Two
Kayla

Kayla reached for her cell phone on her desk as it vibrated. She'd been working in the same position since lunch and only just realized how stiff she had gotten.

Stretching, she smiled as she noticed Evan's name on the screen. Her silent business partner had become less and less silent lately, but she found she didn't mind as much as she thought she would.

"Hello?" she answered.

"Hey. How's it going?" he asked.

"Just knocking some things out at the office. You?" Evan called once a week at minimum and checked in on how things were going. Lately, it was closer to daily.

"Oh, good. I actually wanted to get things set up for me and my friends again." He sounded nervous and she couldn't resist the smile.

"Which one of you is the victim this time?" Kayla teased. There were five of them to go through this blind date scheme they'd set up.

It was out of the ordinary to have people set up on a date in her restaurant. It was usually about letting the app find you a good match, but she'd made an exception for him and his friends only.

"I get to go second since it was my idea," Evan explained.

Her stomach dropped. A heavy weight settled in it, stealing her smile and her words.

"Kayla?" Evan asked when she didn't say anything.

She cleared her throat. "Sorry about that. I got distracted."

"No problem. What do you think?"

Ha. What did she think? She thought this was a very bad idea. "Umm, sure. I can set that up for you. When did you want to start, and who's going to be sending over matches?" Last time Evan had coordinated everything with her, but he couldn't be the point on this if he was the one doing the dating.

"I think it'll be Jake. He's already done it, after all." Evan gave a laugh but it sounded forced.

She took a settling breath before replying. "You know you don't have to do this, right?"

"It's not that I don't want to. I am more concerned it won't work." His voice was quiet, something rare from her loud, confident friend.

"Do you want to talk first?" she offered.

"Nah, I've got this. Can you get it set up? I already did the account thing on my end, so it's just letting the dates come through."

She knew that. "I know. I'll make sure I get them. Pass my email along to Jake, and I'll make sure it gets set up when the women come through." She tried to keep the emotion out of her voice. Truthfully, she wasn't sure why it was there in the first place. "I think you set your profile up a while ago; you might want to go through it and make sure nothing needs updating on the questionnaires."

"Ha! I knew you were going to say that, so I did it already."

She forced a smile into her voice. "Look at you. Must be more excited than you are letting on."

"Everything okay with you?" he asked instead of acknowledging her comment.

"Of course. Why wouldn't it be?" Apparently she wasn't hiding her confusing emotions well.

"I don't know. You sound...off?" he elaborated.

"Probably just because it's been a long day."

"Don't work too hard."

"You know me," she said in an attempt at a joke.

Evan blew out a breath. "I do. That's why I said it."

"Funny."

"Let's do lunch tomorrow?"

"I'll get back to you on it. Let me get this all set up. Maybe you'll have new plans by then." That thought punched her in the gut without warning.

Evan laughed. "I'll still have time to get lunch with you, regardless."

She gave a noncommittal hum. "Let me get this set up and I'll text you when it's done so you can make sure it's good from your end."

"Okay. Thanks Kayla."

They ended the call, and she dropped the phone onto her desk. Evan dating wasn't something she thought about often, on purpose.

She loved hanging out with him, and his business advice was great, but she couldn't bring herself to attempt more with him. If things didn't work out, she'd lose the friend she had and potentially the partner in her business.

What she wanted and what she was going to do were at war, yet again. Evan tied her up in knots sometimes.

They'd get really flirty and there had been times when she thought that he was going to be the one to make a first move and kiss her, but then something would happen to pull them back. It was usually her.

Fear kept her immobilized when it came to Evan, and now she was going to have to let him move on. That was her big problem—she didn't want to.

Her phone vibrated again and she answered it without reading the display. Any distraction at this point was a good one.

"Hey!" Lauren's chipper voice came through the speaker.

"Hi, Lauren. How can I help you?" Kayla scrambled for a pen and got ready to write whatever Lauren wanted down.

"Well," she dragged. "I was calling because Evan is next out of the men doing the blind dates."

Shit. Just her luck that her distraction from Evan would be about Evan. "I know. He called already."

"He did? I mean of course he did. How are you?" Lauren stammered.

"I'm fine. Why?" Did Lauren know? If she did, who else did? Her heart raced and she stood to pace her small office space.

"You see, when we were there together, I noticed that there was something between you two. I was actually calling to see if you would be Jake's pick for Evan?"

Kayla tripped over her thoughts and nearly fell all the way to the floor. She managed to catch herself on the wall and stand up, leaning her back against it.

She pulled the phone away from her ear and pressed it to her racing heart as she struggled to put her thoughts together. It was a lost cause.

Bringing the phone back to her ear, she swallowed before answering. "I'm not sure that would be the smartest idea."

"I thought you might say that. Can you at least think it over and get back to me? Jake doesn't get to go first, which is bullshit if you ask me. I think it's a great idea. You two have chemistry, and I think you'd be missing out if you didn't act on it," Lauren rambled.

"Sure. I'll let you know something soon." She tried and failed to feign enthusiasm again.

"Hey, no pressure. If you really don't want to, that's fine. I know a few people from the office who would probably go for it if Jake can't come up with anyone."

"Can I let you go? I have another call coming in," Kayla interrupted her.

"Oh, sure! Listen just let me know one way or the other. No pressure," she emphasized.

"I will."

Kayla ended the call and stared down at her phone. She needed a secretary to screen these calls so she could avoid all this.

She dropped down into her chair and flipped her phone to silent. That was quite enough of that for right now.

It wasn't that she didn't want Evan to date. That was inevitable and she'd be a little jealous, sure. She wouldn't do anything to interfere, unless something was wrong. She was better than that.

However, she didn't want to be directly involved in him dating. Was it too much to ask?

She needed a drink, and maybe her own date. Maybe that's what she was missing, a date that wasn't lunch with Evan as a friend.

Kayla shook her head at herself. When would she do that? In the imaginary downtime that she had? No. That wasn't going to solve her problem.

Lauren's offer was tempting, but there was no way she could accept it, or so she tried to convince herself. It would be unethical somehow for her to know who her date was and him not to know.

He'd probably figure it out quickly too, and then she'd have to explain herself. That wouldn't work out for her very well.

There was no way she could commit to a blind date with Evan. Right? She struggled to answer her own inner thoughts with rational ones.

Giving up on trying to make any of the last hour make sense, she sat down and did what she knew best—work. Unfortunately the top item on her list now was Evan's profile.

She bit her lip. What if she made her own and just tested their compatibility? It would be a start, right? If they weren't compatible then maybe it was just lust, and she needed to move on from thinking about him.

Kayla had done all the assessments before, more than once since setting them up. She regularly helped calibrate them to make sure they were still accurate, and she helped to set a baseline of how often people should retake it.

She looked around, making sure no one was about to come into her office before she started. In moments, she had her profile created and had uploaded her most recent assessments. Now it was time to bring Evan's online and see who he matched with first.

Chapter Three
Kayla

In the end, Kayla couldn't bring herself to match their tests and see how compatible they were. She was so worried they'd be incompatible that her stomach had been upset all night.

She planned for a long run this morning to clear her mind while enjoying the scenery and music in her headphones. Getting ready, she headed out her apartment building and began her walk to the park entrance. Running here was a waste of effort with too many people in the sidewalk and stops waiting for a crosswalk light to change.

"Hey!" A man reached out and touched her arm.

"Ah!" She jumped and turned to face whoever had approached.

"I didn't mean to scare you." Evan held his palms up.

Kayla threw a hand over her racing heart and attempted to catch her breath. "You scared me half to death," she fussed.

Evan dropped his hands and looked her over. "I'm sorry. Seriously, I had no idea I would scare you."

Calming down now, she took her headphones off to talk to him. "It's okay. I was just lost in my thoughts, I guess."

"Noted. I thought I would join you for a run this morning. Jake was going to run, but he slept in this morning and I don't want to wait until later to go."

Kayla bit back a sigh. This wasn't what she had in mind for today. "Sure. I'm headed for a long one, though, so feel free to bail at any time."

"I think I can handle it."

Kayla nodded and put her headphones back on. They'd see if he could handle it. Hopefully, he'd fall out and leave her to her thoughts, which were now guaranteed to be only on him.

It wasn't that she didn't want to see him, just not right now. She adjusted her headphones and turned the volume down a bit so she could better hear him if he spoke. Headphones worked best for her to run in. She'd tried the ones that just go in your ear, but they either hurt or would fall out.

Evan was one of few people who didn't tease her about her choice there. It wasn't ever mean from anyone, but it got old. She knew she was the exception to everyone else's preferences.

He ran beside her, keeping pace with her without faltering, trying now and then to talk. Kayla kept her answers short without being rude.

"Damn, Kayla, how long are you planning to run today?" Evan huffed out.

She checked her watch to see how far she'd gone. Four miles—she'd push for an even five. "Another mile to go. You can fall out any time." It wasn't like she'd invited him.

Evan randomly ran with her on the weekends. He'd just show up and join her route, and she'd never cared until today. Her thoughts were in turmoil, and it was hard to focus now that he was there.

"Not a chance. You're stuck with me," Evan joked. "Breakfast after. My treat."

Kayla nodded and tried, again, to focus on her run. She navigated people as she went past them and took in the green scenery around the paved path, looking anywhere but at Evan.

By the last mile, her mood had improved enough to agree to

breakfast. It wasn't like Evan knew he was interrupting the solitude she had wanted when any other time she would have greeted him excited that he wanted to join her.

She stopped and stretched near a bench by the exit of the park. "Where did you want to go?"

Evan huffed and attempted some stretching. "You weren't kidding about a long one."

"I did warn you," she offered him a small smile.

"That you did," he mumbled. "How about the coffee place?"

"Because there's only one?" she joked. There were a million coffee places in the city, but she could guess which one he wanted to go to.

"You know which one."

"Do you?" she teased back. Finished stretching, she took a seat on the bench.

Evan fell onto the bench next to her. "I know where it is," he offered.

"It's called Deja Brew." She shook her head. It was a fun name, one she really liked and couldn't have forgotten if she wanted to.

Evan nodded. "That one."

"Okay. Let's go." She stood and then stuck her hand out to pull Evan up. "The walk will do your muscles some good."

"I don't want to walk any further. Let's take a cab."

Kayla laughed. "Not a chance. You need to cool down, and you should have quit when it was too much."

He turned red. "It wasn't too much at the time. It's more the after effects that are too much."

She threw her head back as she laughed. "Right."

As they exited the park, Evan moved around her, keeping himself between her and the traffic just past the sidewalk. When they passed other people and had to give up their spot on the sidewalk to let them pass, his hand would always rest on the small of her back, keeping her with him and moving.

These little touches and thoughtful things he did always gave her butterflies in her stomach even as she told herself these things were just habits for him. He was probably attentive like this to everyone.

"Grab us a seat and I'll order," he told her as they entered Deja Brew.

She nodded and did just that. The butterflies were back to their steady flutter when he said it. Without a doubt, she knew Evan would come back with both the coffee and the muffin she wanted. That he remembered was what got to her.

She noticed Cade walking in and pulled another chair to their table, expecting his presence. Cade was just a hair taller than Evan but wider, more muscular. Not that Evan was scrawny, but Cade definitely worked to build muscle, where Evan stayed in shape.

He was handsome in his own right, but Evan was her preference. She could appreciate other men, but the one she wanted was him, and him alone. Evan's dark hair and always well-groomed beard did things to her she would never admit out loud.

"Here you go." Evan passed her a cup and a bag.

She opened it, knowing already that it was the banana muffin she would have ordered herself. A sip of the coffee confirmed it was the right order. Not that she even needed to check.

"Where's Cade?" she asked him, looking around.

"Flirting with the barista, as usual." Evan rolled his eyes.

Kayla spotted him, chatting with the barista as Evan had said. The barista moved through the orders, setting coffees on the counter and calling out names while Cade chatted with her.

"He should just ask her out," Kayla noted.

Evan snorted. "Good luck convincing him of that."

"When does he get a blind date turn? Maybe she could be your pick for him?" she suggested, still watching the pair.

Evan looked over and rubbed his beard. "I think that's not a half bad idea." He turned to face her. "Any luck with my profile setup?"

Kayla quickly took a sip of her coffee, prolonging her answer as long as she could. "Almost." She took a bite of her muffin to keep from saying anything else.

"Do you think that when you do, you can open it up like a regular profile too?"

Kayla inhaled so quickly she forgot she was chewing her muffin. Immediately she began coughing, drawing the attention of everyone around her.

Evan was up and patting her back in the blink of an eye, handing her a napkin as he did. She struggled to recover, reaching for her coffee to help wash it down.

"I'm okay," she waved him off through a few final coughs.

He looked like he wasn't sure but eventually moved back to his seat. "You sure?" he asked, concern clear in his eyes.

She nodded. "It just went down the wrong way." She shrugged and hoped she didn't look freaked out.

"Everything okay over here?" Cade joined them.

Kayla gave Cade a smile. "I just forgot how to eat for a second."

"These muffins are delicious though, so if you had to go out on something, at least it was good," Cade joked.

It was weird when she ran into Cade here versus when she saw him anywhere else. At Deja Brew, he was much more relaxed and friendly. Not that he wasn't friendly elsewhere, but it seemed forced and less casual.

"Did you hear that Evan's next?" Cade asked.

Kayla nodded. Pushing her muffin away, she took a tentative sip of her coffee and looked over at Evan.

"I was just asking if she would maybe throw me in the regular dating pool too just in case," Evan explained.

"You have no faith in your friends?" Kayla asked him.

"Cade didn't even pick last time; he pawned it off on his sister."

"Hey! I didn't pawn it off. She had an idea and I let her run with it," Cade said in weak defense.

"All right, gentlemen. Evan, yes, but let's wait until after everyone does their picks so it doesn't try to match you at the same time. Cade, I'm sure whoever you pick will be a good choice, with or without Catherine's help."

Cade winked at her. "I think we all know the right choices to make here."

She didn't respond as she tried to puzzle out what that meant. Did he know what Jake and Lauren had asked her? Ugh, probably. This group was as thick as thieves, and she knew that.

The conversation steered away from dates and she was grateful. They talked business and she focused on her coffee while watching the people pass by the window, lost in her own thoughts.

"Thanks for letting me crash your morning. I need to get back to it." Cade stood and nodded at each of them before leaving.

"Do you think they will actually have some good picks?" Evan asked nervously.

She took a moment to think it over. "Honestly, I think the only person you have to worry about is Luke."

Evan rubbed his beard. "Any chance we can just not do his?"

Kayla laughed. "This wasn't my idea. Your agreement here with your friends is on the line. Besides, even Jake made it through, and look how well it turned out."

"Luke is such an idiot," Evan lamented.

He wasn't wrong. "He's young. Eventually, he will grow up and it will be different." She hoped anyway. She knew plenty of men that never grew up.

They both stood and walked to the trashcan, clearing their mess. Evan held the door for her and again his hand rested on her back as he guided her out the door. As a strong woman, it should bother her that he felt the need to do that, but instead, she repressed a shiver of awareness.

"I'm headed home now to shower and get a little work done," she told him as they walked.

"Don't work too hard."

"Oh please, like you aren't going to do the same thing."

"Maybe you should try a date, too? We could do a double date thing?" Evan was full of ideas today, and she didn't want to hear anymore.

Ha! Absolutely not. "I don't think that's a good idea."

"You could come witness the terrible woman that Luke will pick for me."

Kayla rolled her eyes. "The woman won't be terrible, just...flirty."

"That's one word for her," Evan muttered.

She took a breath and reminded herself that he was her friend and she wanted him to be happy. "You have to go into this with an open mind or it won't work at all," she reminded him.

"I just want something like Jake and Owen have. I know that's weird for a man to want a relationship, but I do."

"It's not weird. I assume that's why most of your friends agreed to this." She wasn't sure why Luke had agreed except that the rest had.

"Maybe."

She parted ways with him at her building and had never been happier to return to her apartment alone. It was time to get Evan's profile set up, and then she could ignore this whole topic for a while as she waited to hear from everyone with their date suggestions.

Chapter Four
Evan

As Cade had predicted, Luke's pick came through before the week was over. Evan had tried to chat with her on the app, but she hadn't accepted.

Kayla's restaurant and blind dating app had been a stroke of genius. It allowed for more than a blind date, and if the dates chose, they could chat inside the app using only their first initial if both parties agreed. She said most people actually chose that option, taking the time to get to know each other a little before their date.

The fact that this woman didn't want to chat with him made him more nervous. According to Jake, the woman kept trying to touch him under the table and asked a lot of personal questions about money, making it clear what she was interested in.

He tried to push the dread down, but as he got ready for his date Thursday evening, he couldn't keep it at bay. There was no excitement for tonight at all, only fear of what he was about to run into.

Kayla had told him to keep an open mind, but it was hard when you knew Luke. He was a jokester, making it clear he was the youngest of their group with everything he did.

He looked in the mirror and straightened his silver tie before running a hand over his beard. He'd been considering shaving it, but hadn't brought himself to doing it yet. Shaving was a hassle when your hair grew as quickly as his did. It was close to a twice daily thing when he did try to stay shaved.

Shrugging on his jacket, he pushed his thoughts away. His date wouldn't see him tonight anyway unless for some reason they hit it off so well they decided to meet after. The entrances were separate at the restaurant; one person came in on one side and another on the other, keeping your date from ever seeing you if you didn't want them to.

After the date, both parties had to agree to meet or they wouldn't at all and would either try another date, and chat in the app if they wanted, or they would be unmatched and no one would ever know who they were.

The dinner would be in complete darkness consisting of a salad and drinks. It was the one thing he'd pushed against with Kayla, but in the end, she'd won that they wouldn't have more of a menu. Since the guests could barely see their food, they wouldn't know if they got the right thing, or it was cooked right, she reasoned.

The restaurant wasn't really for food; it was for dates. If people wanted to meet, then they could always go out again after. Or, in his case, probably go home and order a pizza.

Evan headed out to his car and made his way to the restaurant. He'd asked Kayla earlier today for her thoughts on the date, but she'd remained tight lipped, so other than the fact that Luke had chosen this woman for him, he had no idea who he would be meeting.

As he pulled up to the restaurant, meeting the valet and handing over his keys, he took a few steadying breaths before going in. It was an entirely different perception to come in as a date instead of as a partner to this business. After a million visits, he thought he knew what to expect, but this was different somehow.

The waiting area was dimly lit and other men waited on the

benches that lined the entryway. After letting the hostess know he was there, he took a seat and waited for his turn.

He knew how it would work, but when they called his name and he was led into darkness, he barely contained his own nerves. Between the darkness and the anxiety over Luke's choice, he wanted to bolt.

The server explained the process, but Evan tuned him out completely, working to stay calm. After a few beats, the server took Evan's hand and rested it on his shoulder to follow him through the restaurant to his seat.

As he walked, the only light he saw was from the glow of the tables, which was enough to see where your plate and drink were, but not enough to illuminate your face. Keeping identities secret was paramount here, and while the concept was great and the business did well, he admitted it was bizarre as a customer.

Jake had explained it would be, but Evan had brushed him off. Thankfully, he'd also explained that it was less weird each time.

"Here is your table, sir." The server took his wrist, moving his hand from the man's shoulder and placing it on the table. "Your date is here and should be with your shortly."

It was strange how alert he was to sounds and was completely aware that the server had moved away, despite not being able to see him. He was here first, which gave him a moment to compose himself before she joined him.

A few minutes later, the server returned, giving directions to his date. She sat across from him and took a minute to get settled.

"I'll be right back with your food and drinks." They had to order on the app so everything was ready for them when they got there. It wasn't like they could read a menu in the dark.

"This is ridiculous," the woman muttered across from him.

He pretended not to hear and introduced himself. "I'm E, it's nice to meet you, kind of," he joked. Everyone kept their voices soft as the darkness made everything louder than normal.

"This is insane. I didn't think it would actually be completely dark," she said, too loudly, hushing the conversations around them.

"It's not so bad," Evan encouraged.

"Sure. You didn't waste a full face of makeup and a good hair day to sit in the dark," she complained.

He was shocked. Never in all his imaginings of how this date would go did he think that he would have someone who didn't want to be here.

"Your food is here. I am going to sit it in front of you and the table will glow, letting you see where your food and drinks are."

The server set everything in front of them and made sure they were able to locate it before he left them to some privacy again. Evan wanted to beg him to stay.

"So," he started. "How was your day?"

"Well, I spent most of it getting ready for this date." She sounded disgusted.

He wanted to ask her why she had agreed to even go on a date if all she was going to do was complain, but held it in. "I'm sure you look great."

"For all you know I could be the ugliest person you ever met. Or you could be. This is nonsense." She continued her complaining and Evan tried to decide how to tactfully tell her to lower her voice. "I can't believe anyone would agree to come here."

"It's not for everyone," he admitted. "If you're uncomfortable, I wouldn't be offended if you wanted to leave. I understand."

"Oh, thank God. Let's get out of here."

"Sorry, I didn't mean to mislead you. If you would like to leave, that's okay. I am going to finish my salad before I do." He probably wouldn't eat any of it, but he wanted to let her down gently.

"Fine. We can play this game, and I'll eat a salad here before we leave," she huffed. He imagined she rolled her eyes at the same time.

He didn't know for sure, had no way of knowing, but she seemed the type to cause a scene if he flat out told her he wasn't interested.

Instead, he took a bite of his salad and tried to make the best of the situation.

"It's pretty good," he told her.

"Sure." She definitely rolled her eyes that time. "Whenever you're ready, we can leave this place, maybe go to yours."

Thankfully, he had already swallowed his food or he would have spit it at her in surprise. "Actually, I don't think this is going to work."

"Absolutely not!" She rose her voice and the entire restaurant went quiet. "I have spent the day getting ready for you, and I am not about to go home alone."

"Excuse me, ma'am." The server appeared. "I'm going to have to ask you to lower your voice."

"This place is ridiculous. What am I supposed to do, whisper?" She was shouting now, and Evan imagined that had she been standing, she would have been stomping her feet.

"Ma'am, if you do not lower your voice, you will be asked to leave," the server told her.

Evan would have to remember to ask Kayla who his server was and thank him personally later for handling this.

"Oh, so you all just want me to leave? Must be nice to have tons of money and be able to make your date walk out without even treating her to a decent night out!" She grabbed for something, he assumed her purse, and as she did, her drink fell over. "Whatever, maybe rich boy here can help you clean it up."

This was worse than any scenario he could have made up. Absolutely terrible. She continued to yell about how horrible it was here even as her voice faded.

He waited for the server to return to the table before attempting to stand.

"I'm very sorry about that, sir," he said, leading Evan out.

"You handled it better than I could have. Thank you for that."

"Indeed, sir. Ms. Kayla would like to talk to you, if you have time." He led Evan back into the waiting area, waiting with him as his eyes adjusted to the light.

"I'll head up there in just a moment." He reached in his pocket and pulled out his wallet, handing the server a hundred dollar bill. "I appreciate your assistance back there."

"I can't take that. We don't work for tips here."

Evan blinked at the man. "You know who I am, right?" He didn't often say that to anyone.

The server nodded.

"Consider it a bonus then, for a job well done," Evan pressed.

The other man finally took the money and slipped it in his pocket. "Thank you, sir."

"Thank you."

The server went back behind the heavy curtain that kept the light out of the dining room, and Evan headed for the stairs. After he talked to Kayla, he was going to give Luke a piece of his mind.

"You're done already?" Kayla looked up as he entered her office.

"You didn't hear?" he asked, dropping into a chair.

She arched a brow at him. "Hear what?"

"Oh, just my date caused a scene and shouted her way out of the dining room, knocking her drink over in the process."

Kayla's mouth fell opened and he smiled at being able to stun her into silence, something that didn't happen often.

"Also, don't be mad. I tipped my server for dealing with that disaster and kind of used who I was to make him take it."

She laughed. "I'm not mad. I might be if you weren't you, but the staff knows you." She shut her laptop and focused on him. "What the hell happened?"

He explained the very short date to her, and she focused on every word. He loved that about her. Kayla was a busy woman, but she always paid attention to whoever she was talking to, rarely multi-tasking her way through conversations. It made him, and probably everyone else she talked to, feel important to her.

Before he'd gone in with her on this restaurant, he had considered asking her out. He hadn't as he didn't mix business and pleasure, and the idea of this restaurant was too good to turn down.

Then he'd gotten to know her and everything had changed. He regretted never asking her out and seeing what could have been between them, but she didn't seem interested. It was a shame. He imagined whatever might happen between them would be explosive, in a good way.

"Hello?" Kayla waved her hand at him.

He realized he had zoned out. "Sorry, lost in my thoughts for a minute."

"Penny for them?"

"Just thinking of the many things I'm going to do to Luke." It was better than telling her the truth.

"Leave him be. I think he thought this was going to go better than it did," she told him. "He wasn't laughing when he called or anything and was very specific in his information."

He thought it over and shook his head. "Doesn't matter what he might have thought. I know Luke, and this was never going to go well."

"Nothing is going to go well if you go into it thinking that," she reminded him.

He scratched his cheek and considered how the next one might go. At least the worst one was out of the way. "Who's next?"

"I'll set it up later, and you'll get a notification in the app. Don't be dramatic."

"I'm not being dramatic. That was miserable. Ask your staff about it later."

"Be that as it may, you have to be more positive going in."

"I tried. I really did. I couldn't have even guessed this would happen."

She shook her head at him. "I'm really sorry it didn't go well." She opened her laptop up again and typed a few things. "It looks like the manager has already banned her from the system, so at least no one else will go through it."

"Glad I could help with that," he said sarcastically. "I'm going to head home. I'll talk to you later."

"It will get better, Evan."

"Mm-hmm."

He let himself out and made his way home, calling Luke several times. To no one's surprise, he didn't answer. At least it was over. He'd have to trust Kayla that it would get better.

Chapter Five
Evan

Evan's leg bounced as he waited for his name to be called. It was his second blind date, and it had only been two days since the disastrous first one.

Luke had avoided him for the last two days, no doubt knowing how the date went and that Evan was pissed. Or he'd just disappeared again, as he sometimes did to deal with family stuff.

He'd only told Jake about how terribly the date had gone, and only had because Lauren and Kayla had become friends and he figured Kayla would tell her anyway. Everyone else would find out later at poker.

He really hoped that tonight would go better. It was much busier than it had been on Thursday, and he wouldn't recover the embarrassment if he had to endure another date being escorted out. Granted, no one would know it was him and his date, but it would be humiliating all the same.

Kayla hadn't even been willing to tell him who had set him up on this date. With any luck it would be Jake's turn. Since he was settled in a relationship, he'd probably have a better pick.

When his name was called, he stood and walked to the curtain.

He had to admit that Jake was right, and it was slightly less weird this time, since he knew what to expect as far as the darkness.

"Your date is already at the table, sir."

Evan recognized the voice as the same server from last time. "I hope for both our sakes that this one is better than my first one."

"Indeed," was the only reply the man gave him as they approached the table.

His date, B, had opted into the chat feature on the app but had never replied to him. Likely busy and this date was short notice, so he'd brushed it off as a timing issue and had just been happy she'd at least been willing to chat.

Evan took his seat and waited for the server to leave before speaking to his date. "Hello. I'm E, you must be B?" It was a lame introduction but it was something to start from.

She giggled, and he was immediately turned off. It was one of those forced giggles that some women thought was cute but was more like nails on a chalkboard to most people.

"I am. This is such a strange experience." More giggles.

Maybe she was just nervous, he tried to convince himself. "It's definitely different. Did you have a good day today?" Small talk wasn't fun, but he couldn't think of a better way to get the conversation going.

"Oh, I didn't do much, just some shopping and brunch with friends. And getting ready for this date, of course." Again with the giggling.

"That sounds like a good time. My day was a little bit of work and then a few other things I had to get done before getting ready."

"What do you do for work?" she asked.

"I'm in consulting." He was intentionally vague. "What about yourself?"

"Work? I don't do that," she scoffed. "My parents have me on a generous allowance, so I don't have to work."

"Oh, umm, how do you spend your time?" He prayed for volunteer work, or anything of substance.

"Mostly shopping and hanging out with my friends. I attend some parties that my father has and sometimes help set those up and tell everyone where to put things. I'm really good at that."

He rubbed his beard and tried not to sigh so she wouldn't hear him.

"Your food has arrived," the server said.

Plates were set in front of them alongside drinks. The server again made sure they could find everything before leaving them to their privacy again.

As he reached for his fork, something touched his leg. He jerked back but didn't say anything.

They continued the small talk, nothing of any substance, for a few minutes until something touched his leg again.

"Are you interested in taking me out for drinks after?" B asked, forcing her voice to be sultry.

"I don't think I'm up for drinks tonight. Sorry."

"A man with a plan. I like it. Should we just head straight back to your place then?" Her fake sultry voice held all the innuendo it could.

B's foot inched higher up his leg, even as he tried to shuffle out of her reach.

"I'm not sure what you were led to believe, but I'm not looking for someone to just sleep with. I'm looking for a relationship, and that means getting to know the person before anything like that." Being gentle hadn't worked well last time, so he'd try the direct approach with her.

Another annoying giggle. "What better way to get to know someone than naked and in bed?"

"I don't think this is going to work out." He didn't end it with a fake apology this time. Evan wasn't sorry, he was frustrated.

"Why?" She seemed genuinely confused.

Evan sighed. "I reached out to you on the app to try to get to know you. I'm just not looking for sex right now."

Her toes grazed his dick, and it was more than he was willing to take. Her foot hadn't even touched him in the last minute or two, but somehow she'd honed in directly on her target.

Reaching down, Evan removed her foot. "I'm not sure why you think that I'm going to change my mind, but I assure you, I'm not interested."

He reached over and pressed the button at the end of the table, signaling to the server that he needed something. She pouted; while he couldn't see her, he could hear her and he needed to get out of here.

"Can I help you?" the server arrived.

"Yes, please. Our date is over and I'd like to make my way out."

"Yes, sir. Hold your hand out and I will assist you. Ma'am, I will return shortly to help you as well."

Evan followed him out and let out a huge sigh of relief as the heavy curtain closed behind him.

"What is your name, again?" Evan asked.

"It's Nigel, sir."

That was unique enough to remember. How had he missed it twice? "Thank you, Nigel, for helping me out once again. I'm gonna to head up to Kayla's office."

"Of course." Nigel nodded and let the curtain fall between them.

Evan took the stairs up to meet Kayla to give himself time to think. This wasn't going well, and he was having second thoughts on doing another date at all.

"Knock, knock," he said as he walked through Kayla's open office door.

"Evan?" She looked down at her watch. "That was...quick."

He gave a harsh laugh and settled into a chair. "Felt like forever."

"Oh no." She slid her laptop to the side and focused on him. "Was it that bad?"

"If you count someone's foot making unwanted contact with my dick as bad, then yeah," he lamented.

Kayla threw a hand over her mouth, and it took him a second to realize she was laughing.

"Seriously?" he asked, not as shocked as he wanted to be by her laughter.

She struggled to compose herself before talking. "I'm sorry. I guess you just caught me off guard. I'm also pretty sure I've never heard you say anything crass before, ever."

Crass? What the hell had he said that was crass? "What?" he managed.

"Dick. You've never said it before while I was around. You're always so proper. I guess this date really got to you."

Well, maybe he hadn't. It wasn't like there were a lot of opportunities to say anything like that around her. "It was awful. I don't know if I can do anymore."

"Oh, don't be like that. There's got to be something better waiting. Besides, Jake had a few before Lauren that didn't go well either."

"I don't think he had two that were this bad."

"Maybe talk to him and ask?"

"I've talked to him, a lot, about this." He had, as Jake was the only one with experience. "Maybe dating just isn't in the cards for me right now." Or ever.

Kayla bit her lip as she studied him. It was like she was making a decision before she finally spoke. "I doubt that your next one will be that bad. I think you should give it at least one more shot."

That got his interest. "What do you know?"

"That's not how this works, I keep telling you that." She scolded him complete with an arched brow to prove her point.

"I should get some perks. This was my idea, and I'm a partner after all." He knew she wouldn't give on this, but he wanted any kind of reassurance he could get.

Kayla picked up her pen and started clicking it as he knew she did when she was nervous, but she didn't say anything.

"I give up. Also, I've yet to have a full salad here because these dates are bad so I don't even know what a real date is like here." He was hungry. "Do you want to go get some pizza or something?"

She giggled, and it struck him that she did that now and then and it didn't bother him at all when she did it.

"I don't think so, not tonight. I'm also not going on a run in the morning. The weather is supposed to be crappy so I'm staying in and using the treadmill."

Now he felt like he was being blown off. At some point in their partnership, he'd started viewing Kayla as more than a partner—he saw her as a friend. It had been a while now, but she'd not blown him off so directly before, and now he was confused.

"Okay. I'll just get out of your hair then." He stood and turned to leave.

"Evan?" Kayla's voice was quiet and unsure. "I'm not upset with you. I'm just busy tonight, and I didn't want you trying to meet me for a run tomorrow."

"Okay." He shrugged. Did it matter? "It's not a big deal. Today has been so long, and I think I'm just drained."

"Understandably. Don't think I don't want to hang out with you though. I don't want to fight with you over something so trivial." Kayla explained herself, and stood, coming towards him. "Don't be mad."

"I'm not mad. I think I'm just exhausted." His brain had been too busy stressing over this date, and then there was the date itself that wasn't helping things.

"It'll work out, Ev." She brought her hand up to his chest, stopping just short of touching him before hesitating.

He couldn't resist himself and took half a step forward, making her touch him. Why couldn't he find this kind of ease of talking to anyone else? With someone who wanted him?

"Be careful, Ev. I'll see you soon, I'm sure," Kayla said before dropping her hand and going back to her desk, putting distance between them.

It wasn't until he was halfway down the stairs that it even occurred to him that she had called him Ev twice. She had never done that before. Now his already tired brain had even more to figure out.

He made his way home and ordered dinner before changing and relaxing on his sofa. What did Kayla's nickname mean for him? Did it mean anything? He had no sure way of knowing without asking her, and he didn't want to do that.

His phone suddenly went off from a text from the lady herself.

Kayla: *Your next date is in the system.*

Evan: *I really hope this one goes better.*

Kayla: *Me too.*

It would also be good for business if he was able to manage a successful relationship from this. Showing that as a partner, he was also willing to use the service and it worked would be a great story they could use.

Chapter Six
Kayla

Kayla hadn't thought either of those dates would go well for Evan, but she hadn't even imagined they'd be that bad. Luke's choice wasn't a surprise for incompatibility, but Ryker's had been. She expected better from his friends than this.

Although, Ryker hadn't been laughing like an idiot when he gave her his choice like Luke had. Of course, maybe he didn't know what she would be like. She was going to choose to believe that was the truth versus anything else. Positive intent should always be assumed, unless you're laughing like a teenage boy when you do something.

While he'd been in her office, reliving his awful date, she'd made her choice. She was going to experience the date herself and go out with Evan. The only thing left to do was to let Lauren know she was in and then set it up.

She wondered if Evan would be mad at her deception, but if it went well, even if things didn't work between them, at least Evan would have a good date. She'd do her best to make sure of it.

Setting aside her thoughts, she called Lauren to let her know.

"Hey girl," Lauren answered.

"Umm...I'm in," Kayla told her.

There was a pause before Lauren spoke. "You're in for what? Oh...you're going to go on a date with Evan?"

Kayla nodded and then smacked her palm to her forehead. They were on the phone, so Lauren couldn't see. "Yes."

"Ah! I'm so excited! I think this is going to go so freaking great! You guys have amazing chemistry."

Kayla wondered how she would have picked up on that but didn't ask. It was probably better that she didn't know. "I'm going to set it up. Am I calling this Jake's choice, or do you get your own?"

"This is Jake's. He's excited too. This is going to be great."

"Or this is going to blow up in my face and Evan is going to hate me." She sighed. That was the worst-case scenario.

"Kayla, don't think things like that. You sound like Evan about his dates already, and you haven't even been on one."

Her heart fell into her stomach. "Is he there?"

"No, he called Jake on his way home."

"Do you, umm, do you think I should chat with him in the app?" She was getting nervous even thinking about it.

"Definitely. Flirt with him a little. Do and say the things you won't say to him in person when he knows it's you."

She'd already done that today by accident. *Ev*—she didn't even know where that had come from, but it felt right at the time. She wasn't sure if he'd noticed; he hadn't said anything about it.

"Okay. I'll let you know how it goes."

"This is going to be amazing."

"Night, Lauren."

"Night. Keep me posted!"

Kayla ended the call and pulled her computer back over in front of her. *In for a penny, in for a pound.* She pulled up her test and put it in, creating her account.

A fake name wasn't needed. K was vague enough not to question it. With her profile set, she compared their tests to rank their compatibility.

While that ran, she texted Evan to let him know she had set up his next date. She kept it short, and thankfully, he didn't ask any questions about it.

Her computer dinged letting her know the test had completed. Her hands shook as she turned to look at it. She didn't know if it was fear that they might not be compatible or fear that they might be.

Kayla's jaw dropped as she took in the results. It said they were a perfect match. She'd never seen that before on any of other tests.

Solidifying what she already knew, she set up the rest of her profile on the app then pressed the button to allow chats from her date. She didn't know if she could actually keep this a secret from Evan or not, but for now, she was going to embrace her anonymity and flirt with Evan.

The restaurant closed while she was still contemplating her life choices. Grabbing her laptop and slipping it into the bag she carried back and forth to work, she headed home. Tomorrow, she wasn't planning to work, but she couldn't bring herself to leave it behind, ever.

Evan had tried for months to upgrade her to a desktop computer when he'd first come on as a partner, but she'd resisted. There was something comforting about having all the information she could need in one spot.

Not that it wasn't all in the cloud anyway, but it was mind over matter and this is what she wanted. The only thing she'd conceded was to get a monitor for her office so she could have a bigger screen. She rarely used it.

By the time she made it home, her mind had bounced around so many different ways this could turn out. As long as Evan didn't find out what she had done, it would be okay. Despite the match test results, it was unlikely they would get to the meeting part, and maybe she was just helping Evan be less stressed about dating by not having a bad one, or so she was trying to convince herself.

It was a win-win scenario. She got to find out if they were actually good together while dating and didn't have to suffer through the potential ruin of their friendship and partnership in the process.

Evan

The strange thing was, Evan was to be a silent partner and neither one of them had meant to get into a friendship at all. When she'd first met him, she'd just been pitching her restaurant to his company, looking for startup funding.

Not only had Evan agreed to fund her company, instead of a loan, he'd offered to back her as a silent partner. He was absolutely behind her idea and had offered any advice he had to give to help her launch.

It hadn't all been smooth sailing; they'd had some arguments. Sometimes she won, sometimes he did. However, she could honestly say that unlike other relationships of any kind that she'd had, neither of them seemed to be keeping score of who won. She wasn't at least, and Evan had never given her any indication that he was.

She showered and crawled into bed, debating if it was wrong to reach out to Evan, either as herself or ask K in the app. It was late though and probably not the best idea.

Instead, she'd flipped on a movie and half watched it as she thought about Evan. If it did work out, would he be so mad that it didn't matter? Was there a point that she should pull out?

There were too many questions that she had no answers for, and she hated it. She was perpetually organized and liked everything to fit neatly in its own little space. Evan never had.

Maybe that was her attraction to him. Aside from the obvious, of course. The man was gorgeous. Even back in the first meeting she had with him, she'd found her mouth go dry as he walked in.

It still happened sometimes. The last two nights after these dates when he'd shown up in her office, he'd taken her breath away for a moment before she recovered.

Kayla stretched out in her bed and flipped off the movie. She had no idea what had happened, so trying to pay attention at this point was moot.

Her phone dinged and she reached over and grabbed it, already knowing it was Evan. He had his own tone. She was a mess.

Evan: *Are you sure this one will be better? At least be honest about that part.*

Kayla: *I don't think it will be as bad as the other ones.*

Evan: *I'm sorry I was an ass earlier. I have no excuse.*

Kayla: *You're stressed. It's okay. No hard feelings.*

Evan: *I shouldn't take it out on you though. That's wrong and I'm a jerk for it.*

Kayla: *You're already forgiven. Don't think about it anymore.*

Evan: *Can't. Don't like that I upset you.*

Kayla: *You didn't.*

Evan: *She wants to chat, in the app. Do you think I should?*

Kayla: *I think that's up to you. You seemed disappointed the other women didn't chat with you, though.*

Evan: *I'm a mess.*

Kayla: *No you're not, you're just overthinking it.*

Evan: *I'll let you get some sleep. Sorry for bugging you.*

Kayla: *Goodnight, Evan.*

Evan: *Sweet dreams, Kayla.*

She stared at the messages and wondered what had changed between them and what it meant. *Sweet dreams* was definitely new from him. Maybe she needed to take her own advice and stop over-thinking things.

Kayla dropped her head back on the pillow after putting her phone down. She was the one who was a mess. There was no way she'd make it through this.

Chapter Seven
Kayla

Sunday morning was gloomy and gray. Despite the fact that Kayla knew she'd feel more awake if she got on the treadmill, she ordered breakfast to be delivered and curled up with a warm blanket on the sofa.

Movies weren't something she often took the time to watch. If anything, she'd rather be reading, but she rarely made time for that either. Today was about turning off her brain and getting lost in a happily-ever-after.

She took her time picking one that she knew was just going to be a feel-good type of movie as she waited for her French toast and latte to arrive. Not once did she think about Evan...at least not on purpose.

Her phone chimed and she grabbed it expecting her delivery only to find that Evan had messaged her through the app. It was as though she had conjured him up by trying to convince herself not to think of him. She stared at it for too long before finally opening the message.

E: Good morning. I hope it's not too early for you. I just wanted to say hi.

God, the man was a gentleman in all things he did, even an

opening text with a stranger. And why wouldn't he be good at reaching out to someone? It's not like he literally did that for a living.

Kayla sat up straighter and thought about how to respond. It wasn't that she didn't want to, but it was weird knowing that it was Evan, adding a whole different layer of nerves to this blind date thing.

K: I'm up, waiting on some breakfast and coffee. How are you?

There, that was simple, starting a conversation without being weird.

Her food arrived. The idea of having it all cozy and comfy was shot now that Evan was messaging her, so she took it to the table to eat like a civilized person. Pulling off the lid to her latte, she inhaled it deeply and moaned over it. This place had the best ones, but they were so full of sugar and junk that she rarely let herself order it, usually choosing something a lot lighter.

E: I'm glad I didn't wake you.

E: What's for breakfast?

Kayla smiled down at her phone. It was so like Evan to go to her mention of food. For some reason, that was his definition of small talk and had been as long as she'd known him. It was probably the main reason he fought her on just serving salad.

K: French toast and a latte.

She sent the message and then groaned. Now if she talked to Evan, she had to remember not to tell him what she'd ordered for breakfast. This was going to be a challenge. Not that it would be too weird that two people ordered the same thing for breakfast, but she didn't want to make him suspicious either.

E: Oh nice. I had bacon and eggs today.

K: That sounds good too.

It was awkward, there was no way around it. Worse than first-date awkward because she knew him. For the millionth time, she regretted agreeing to this.

E: So, what are you planning to do on this gray day?

K: I was going to watch a movie and eat my breakfast.

E: Was?

K: Now I'm talking to you, lol.

E: I didn't mean to interrupt your morning.

K: It's not like it was anything important. I don't mind being interrupted, and it's nice to hear from you before our date.

E: Have you done this before?

K: I have not. You?

She wondered what he would say in response to that. Obviously, she knew he had done this twice over, but if he was a smart man, he wouldn't go too much in detail.

E: I have. Twice.

K: They didn't work out?

E: Some of my friends can be jerks.

K: I'm sorry.

E: Not your fault at all. You're the first person I've been able to chat with on here, and I'm glad you accepted that option.

She didn't know what to say so she let the conversation pause while she took another long sip of her latte before picking her phone back up again.

K: Sorry, food got here. What's your plans for today?

Taking a bit of the fluffy French toast, she waited on him to reply. He hadn't told her what he was going to do today, so at least it was just a normal conversation and not her thinking up something to ask and already knowing the answer. That made it a little better.

E: I normally go running with a friend, but the weather stopped that, so I don't really have any plans.

She smiled down at her phone at the mention of friend. She thought of him as a friend too, but it was nice to have confirmation that she was more than a colleague when he talked to other people.

K: Yeah, this weather makes it a hassle to do anything.

Kayla looked out her windows at the still gray sky despite it being late morning. She watched the rain drip down the glass. She missed her run, even with Evan when she couldn't shake him from her mind like last weekend. It was throwing off her routine, and she didn't like it.

E: A movie suits this day. What were you going to watch?

K: Nothing in particular. Just scrolled through the app and landed on anything with a happy ending.

They chatted away the morning, talking about nothing and everything all at once. Evan was careful not to ask anything that might reveal who she was, and she only slipped up once asking about his job. He nicely told her that was off-limits.

After a while, she forgot who she was talking to. It was a fun exchange of just two people trying to get to know each other, and she learned some things she didn't know about Evan from before, like how much he hates peas. Such a strange thing to feel so strongly about.

As the morning gave over to afternoon, there was no stopping their conversation. By late afternoon, Evan moved their conversation towards their first date.

E: What night is good for you to "meet" in person.

K: Honestly, I can make almost any night work.

E: How's Thursday work for you?

K: Perfect!

She was surprised he hadn't wanted to meet sooner. Probably nerves because of the last two dates, though.

Kayla went in the app and accepted Evan's invitation for a date on Thursday.

E: All set up.

K: Just accepted. Looking forward to it.

E: Me too. It's been great getting to know you today.

K: Same.

E: I'm going to take a break from my phone though and visit with a friend.

Wondering who, Kayla was taken aback at the abrupt end to the conversation, wondering if she had said something wrong.

E: If it's okay, I'd like to text you tomorrow?

K: That sounds great to me.

E: I have to work so it won't be consistent, just fair warning.

K: Understood.

Her work wasn't as demanding on her time as far as not being able to text unless there was something big going on, which was rare.

E: Have a good night.

K: You too.

Tossing back the blanket and standing up from the couch, she stretched before walking to the window. The rain hadn't let up today at all, but she felt better than she had when she first started talking to E on the app.

Things had gone surprisingly well. She did wonder who he was going to visit today. Probably Cade, she decided. No real reason, just her best guess.

Her phone rang, and she walked back to the couch, searching for where it had went when she moved the blanket. Finding it quickly, she saw Evan calling. Only a moment's indecision stopped her before she finally answered.

"Hey, Evan." She forced too much cheer into her voice and then shook her head at herself.

"You good? You sound, weird," Evan teased.

"Weird how?" Kayla did her best to sound normal.

"I don't know. Anyway, what are you doing?"

Oh no, why was he asking that? "Not much, just laying around."

"I want to talk to you about the next date. I'll bring dinner."

Please no. "I don't know, Evan. You constantly try to get me to give you more information, and it's a little exhausting." At least that was true.

"I'm sorry. I don't have any questions about that. I talked to her all day, and I want your opinion on some things. I'll be by soon, with dinner."

He ended the call before she could protest again. Sounds like this was happening whether she wanted it to or not. Shit.

Chapter Eight
Kayla

Kayla had barely processed Evan's phone call. She was still sitting, dumbfounded, looking at it when there was knocking on the door. She was his friend he needed to go see? No way. There was just no way. He had a tight group of friends already—she surely didn't rank above them. What did it mean if she did?

Pushing that thought away, she opened the door to a grinning Evan holding up takeout bags.

"Let me in, I brought carbs." He slid past her and into the kitchen. "Carbs don't count when they're gifts."

She rolled her eyes and tightened her robe that she forgot she was wearing. "I'll be right back, let me...umm...get dressed." Gesturing to herself, she bolted.

"You don't have to change, this is your apartment," Evan called after her.

Safe inside her bedroom, she leaned against the door and let out a sigh. She looked a mess and could guarantee it without looking in the mirror, yet she'd opened the door. There had been almost ten minutes for her to put herself together and instead she'd sat on the couch like an idiot staring at her phone.

Oh no! The phone, the messages. What if he texts K while he's here? She slid the switch over to silent and dropped it on her bed. It was literally the first day, and she was already going to screw it all up.

Quickly, she tossed her robe and opted for some yoga pants and a loose-fitting top before throwing her hair in a messy bun. Workout wear was at least something that Evan had seen her in before. It was hardly stylish, but at least she was more put together than five minutes ago.

She splashed her face with water and debated a bit of makeup before deciding against it. It wasn't like he'd never seen her without it. At least she didn't end up watching a movie that made her cry or else she'd be all red and puffy. Small miracles.

"You coming to eat?" Evan called from the hallway.

Deciding she might as well get it over with, she opened the bedroom door and ran right into him. "Sorry," she muttered.

Evan's hands had caught her and were holding her shoulders. She was inches from his face and her gaze now eye level with his lips, something she shouldn't have noticed. Something she couldn't avoid noticing.

"Are you good?" Evan asked. He dropped his hands and gestured for her to precede him down the hall. "You didn't have to change. If I'd have known you were in a robe, I wouldn't have bothered to get dressed either."

Kayla gave a half laugh. "If you had decided to let me know you were coming over with a little notice, I would have been dressed before you got here." Honestly, he was here a little too fast, with food. "How did you get the food that fast anyway? Rob someone?"

"Nope, I ordered it before I called you," he said as though that was totally normal and handed her a plate.

"What? What if I wasn't home? Or didn't want company?" Just assuming that she was going to be here was a little disappointing. What did that say about her life, or lack thereof?

Evan winked. The man actually winked.

"Come on, we can eat in the living room. I want to talk to you."

She followed him with her plate. "What the hell? Are you dying or something?"

"Shut up. I wouldn't be telling you like this if I was. I don't know if I'd tell anyone to be honest. Maybe just let it happen so no one has to wait for it." He shrugged.

Something was up with him, and she didn't know what the hell it was.

"First, this is too much food." She held up the overflowing plate of a giant burger and entirely too many fries. "And second, if you find out that you're dying and don't tell me, I will bring you back to life and kill you again myself."

Evan's shoulders shook as he laughed around his burger. "You'd bring me back to life and kill me? Do you have the ability to do that, because I can think of better uses for bringing people back from the dead."

"Shut up."

"And this is far from too much food. It's the right amount for burger and fries."

She looked down at her grease-soaked food and grimaced. Then her stomach betrayed her and growled. The French toast was the only thing she'd eaten today.

"See? Admit it. You like this stuff, you're just so caught up on your rabbit food you don't let yourself enjoy anything."

"I enjoy plenty. My life just doesn't revolve around food."

"It doesn't have to revolve around it to enjoy it."

"I enjoy my food." Most of the time. "I appreciate this more when I don't eat it all the time. It makes it that much better. I'm still not going to eat it all."

He raised a brow at her. "Whatever you don't eat, I will."

He probably would too. Who knew where he put it. The man had the best metabolism.

They ate and watched TV until she needed a break. She'd eaten more of her food than she thought she would, and it was a lot of food.

"What did you want to talk about?" she asked, wiping her mouth with a napkin.

Evan set his plate down and turned to her. "I talked to the next girl I'm supposed to date today."

Well, that was not at all what she was expecting. "Oh?" She winced internally—that was the best she could do?

"Yeah. We talked all day, and I think it went really well."

"And?" She needed him to get to the point so they could talk about anything else at all.

"And I need to know what to do." Evan stood and paced the space between the couch and TV. "I don't want this date to go like the last one, so what do I do?"

"Evan, sit down. You're making me nervous. What makes you think this date would go like the others?" she asked. "There's been two dates and they weren't good matches. Honestly, if I didn't know better, I would assume that they were the same person." She tried for casual and added a shrug at the end for effect. "This woman is talking to you, so that's already a difference there. And you talked for a while, you said, so it's got to be a good sign."

Was she a jerk for not coming clean right then? Probably. Was there any way she was going to tell him right now? Nope.

"I guess you're right."

She didn't have to force her grin this time. "I'm always right."

"Can't be true," Evan teased.

"You know it is," she laughed back.

"Okay, so what movie are we watching?" Evan moved closer to her and sat next to her on the couch so they were both directly in front of the TV.

"I didn't invite you for a movie. Or dinner for that matter," she protested as she tried to scoot away from him. Her couch was over-stuffed and it swallowed them a bit, making it hard to adjust without being obvious.

Evan only smiled at her as he grabbed the remote and draped him arm around her shoulders, like this was a normal thing for them. She didn't try to fake anything, but stood and took their plates to the kitchen.

She stood over the sink, letting the water run as she collected her thoughts. It wasn't like she wanted him to leave, but the man was too close for comfort, again.

"If you don't come back soon, I'm going to pick the movie alone," Evan called.

Kayla almost told him she didn't care, but she knew he'd pick something violent, and she really didn't want to watch that. Instead, she turned off the water and went back in the living room.

"Come here, Kayla." Evan patted the cushion next to him.

"You're in my space," she frowned.

"I want to be in front of the TV like you always are."

"Fine, I'll go over here and stretch out." She went to where Evan had been sitting and turned her body to face the TV, stretching her legs out on the chaise.

Evan arched a brow at her but didn't say anything. After a few minutes they settled on a comedy and Evan hit play.

He kept looking over at her while the movie started but still kept his thoughts to himself. After the fourth or fifth time, she'd had enough.

"What?" She rolled her eyes.

"Huh?" Evan feigned innocence.

"Why do you keep looking over at me? Is there food on my face?" Probably not, which made her more confused.

Evan threw a throw pillow at her instead of responding.

"What the hell, Evan?" She kicked her legs off the couch and sat up, tossing it back.

"What the hell, Kayla?" he mocked and tossed the pillow back.

This time when she went to return fire like a freaking middle schooler, Evan was there to stop it.

"Evan!" She wrestled to get the pillow back, intending to whack him with it.

Yanking hard, Evan came tumbling down over her. His body landed on hers, his arms bracing himself, keeping the impact from being too much.

The pillow was next to them, most of his body now flush with hers as they looked at each other, barely inches apart. His eyes searched her face for something before his gaze rested on her lips.

"Kayla," his voice strained.

She wanted him to kiss her as much as she didn't. It was a battle inside of her, and she didn't know which decision she was going on make.

In the end, she was saved from making it as Evan backed away.

"I think I should go. I'll talk to you later." He grabbed his keys off the counter. "Thanks for dinner."

As quickly as he'd barged in, he left, leaving Kayla, still on the couch, more confused than ever.

Chapter Nine
Evan

Somehow, Thursday had snuck up on him and now it was here.

Evan: *Come on, Kayla.*

Kayla: *If I had known you were going to be like this, I would never have agreed to do this.*

Evan: *Give me some kind of hint.*

Kayla: *Go back to work.*

Evan: *Throw me a bone here.*

Kayla: *If you don't leave me alone, I'm going to block you.*

Evan: *No you won't.*

Kayla: *Try me.*

He sighed and dropped his phone on his desk. She was serious and he knew it.

He couldn't help it. He was more nervous for his date tonight than he had been for any of the other dates. Stupidly, he'd thought getting to know his date more before would help, but it was all a lie. Now he didn't know what they were going to talk about.

They'd chatted in that app all week and had covered every topic imaginable. It was great and the conversations were easy, but what did that leave to chat about in the dark tonight?

Evan ran a hand down his face. He needed to wrap up work and get ready to meet her. He wanted to meet her.

He also wanted to talk to Kayla, who had pretty much avoided him sine this weekend. In the middle of all these dates and the chats going great in the app with K, he'd also almost kissed Kayla. What was wrong with him?

If this date didn't go well, he was going to see a therapist, right after he got back from a long vacation. He needed a break from his brain at this point.

"Evan?" His assistant poked her head in his office.

"Yes, Carla?" He forced his annoyance with himself down and tried to focus on her.

Carla was a short motherly woman who had applied for the position when Evan was just starting out. He liked her better than the other applicants at the time, and she had experience so he hired her. Now, she was an integral part of what he did.

He'd promoted her from secretary to assistant just to get her to take a pay raise. She didn't need it, she had told him, but she had eventually conceded. She was pushing well into retirement years but with no kids or family around, he assumed she stayed so she could be needed, and he needed her.

"I was, umm, well, my work is done so I was looking at my phone." She looked at the floor.

He knew she played on her phone sometimes and didn't care as long as there was no work waiting and she never gave him a reason to complain. "And?"

"Well, there's an article that came up, and I thought you should see it."

Ah, that's why she was telling on herself. "I know you look at your phone. You get your work done so I don't mind as long as it doesn't interfere, you know that." He rose and went to the door where she hovered, just short of stepping into his office. "What's the article?"

Carla turned her phone around, facing him.

BLIND DATE RESTAURANT LETS IN ALL KINDS

The bold black headline glared at him. He skimmed the article quickly, catching enough to know it wasn't good news. "Send that to me, now." He handed Carla her phone back.

Evan went back to his desk and immediately called Kayla.

"I'm still not telling you anything," she answered.

"I'm cancelling it." He pulled the phone away from his ear and forwarded the message from Carla over to her. "Check your texts."

"What?" Confusion was clearly in her voice. He heard the phone move. "Oh my God," she whispered.

"I'm on my way over. I haven't read the whole thing. I'll call Catherine and meet you at your office."

"Wh-why? This is on a national site, Evan."

"I know, Kayla. I'll be there shortly."

He grabbed his suit jacket and keys, heading out of his office, when Carla appeared again.

"I called Catherine. She should be calling you," Carla told him.

He paused long enough to make eye contact with her. "You are a saint."

"Shoo." She motioned for him to go.

Carla was always uncomfortable with praise. She claimed she was just doing her job and didn't need recognition for doing what she was supposed to. In reality, he couldn't do half of what he did without her anticipating all his needs before he knew them. Well, he could do it, but it would take longer.

The elevator doors closed as his phone rang. "Catherine," he answered.

"I'll meet you at the restaurant," she told him.

"Thank you." He breathed a sigh of relief. If anyone could help, it would be her.

Catherine didn't reply and the call ended. What was there even to say at this point? They'd discuss it when they got to the restaurant. He wondered if she was going to be offensive or defensive. Whatever path she chose, he trusted Catherine completely.

This wasn't the first time she'd had to help with the restaurant with publicity. Catherine was Cade's sister and the absolute best public relations person he'd ever met, and he'd met more than his fair share in his line of work.

Not that long ago, when Jake and Lauren had first started dating, Lauren's mother sought to exploit the couple—well, Jake specifically, but through Lauren. When they didn't cave, she made up a big story about them and the restaurant. Catherine spun it to their advantage, and it was a great success story for Blind Date.

In the end, Lauren's mother hadn't been able to get her story off as she wanted because they had beat her to it. Cade and Catherine's father had been mad about the relationship because it happened to be the same time that Cade had finally stood up to his father and had caused more trouble. It was a long month.

The drive to the restaurant was short as always, but it felt like it took forever. Pulling up, he barely had the car in park before he tossed his keys to the valet, a service he rarely used here, and ran inside.

It wasn't until he was in the lobby that he remembered his date. He stopped long enough to send her a message.

E: I'm so sorry. I have a work emergency that I can't put off. I'm going to have to cancel.

E: I would love to reschedule if you're still up for it. I'll message you again later.

After sending the last message, he headed for the stairs and Kayla's office. He hated to cancel on K, but he couldn't go on a date right now.

She was pacing behind her desk when he walked in. Her white pants suit turned her into a blur as she moved back and forth.

"Kayla?" he asked as he let himself in.

"Evan?" She blew out a breath and stopped walking for a moment. "What the hell is going on? Why is someone doing this?"

"I don't know. I can promise you, we'll figure it out." He went to her and pulled her in for a quick hug. "Catherine is on her way here, too."

Kayla nodded and then stepped back. "I just don't understand. Who is this anonymous source? And why are they telling people we don't do background checks on people? They're basically implying we let homeless people in for a free meal and a date with a billionaire. We check everyone, Evan." Deflated, Kayla sat down and dropped her head into her hands.

"Breathe. We will figure this out. Has there been any fallout yet?" Evan asked.

Kayla shook her head. "No emails, no calls. I haven't checked to see if anyone cancelled their dates. I should have thought about that already." She grabbed her phone.

Evan reached out and put his hand on hers, stopping her from using the phone. "Don't. Let's see what Catherine says. Besides, one of those cancels was me."

"Oh, Evan. I'm sorry."

"It's okay. This is more important right now."

"Thank you."

He took a seat in the chair across her desk to wait for Catherine. There was sure to be damage control needed, and he wanted to make sure they both knew he was all in on helping fix this. As a "silent partner" he should let her handle it, but it had never really been that way for him when it came to Kayla.

She'd quickly become his friend, and he had helped with this restaurant more than he had with any other business that he'd invested in. Sure, he helped everyone he worked with, but he was a lot less hands-on and involved in the day-to-day operations than he was here.

Evan

Kayla scrambled to stand up and her chair rolled backwards, bumping the wall, even as she rounded her desk. "Catherine!" She went to her friend and wrapped her in a hug. "I'm so sorry to have you do this again."

Chapter Ten
Evan

Friday morning, Evan was back at Blind Date, having barely been gone. There was a press conference scheduled for a few hours from now, and all his friends were on their way to the restaurant.

He grabbed an empty chair and took a seat as Catherine and Kayla talked. He knew what he needed to do today and wasn't concerned about how to answer questions. Kayla was nervous as hell, but she was leaning on Catherine instead of him, which annoyed him more than he liked.

Another annoying thing was there had been no response from K in the app. He hadn't written her again today, but was surprised that she hadn't even acknowledged that he'd canceled the date.

Checking his phone again, he sighed and put it away.

"Evan." Jake slapped him on the back and sat next to him. "Any word on what this is all about?"

"Nothing yet. Catherine's team is on it, threatening to sue if they don't reveal their anonymous source. She seems hopeful we will have an answer today."

"Well, I'd trust her. She knows what she's doing."

Evan nodded. He knew they'd figure it out one way or another. They had grounds to sue as the information was false anyway, but he wanted to know who said it. Then he wanted a damn retraction printed and an apology.

Cade and Ryker joined them a moment later.

"Is Luke coming?" Jake asked.

Ryker nodded. "He's on his way. So is Owen."

It was amazing to have friends that would turn out for you at a moment's notice and be back again in the morning. The plan from Catherine was to present a united front and talk about the dates they had and the ones they planned to go on.

Lauren had joined Catherine and Kayla. Evan watched as the trio chatted over notes, and Kayla took more each time she nodded. He hated that she was going through this.

"I have someone looking into Lauren's mom's whereabouts. I hate to think that this is my mess again, but I need to be sure." Jake told them.

"Catherine is already confirming that it's not the father, but last we spoke, she hadn't been able to one way or the other yet."

"Why would either of them want to start this over again? Jake and Lauren are living together and happy as hell."

Evan shrugged. "We've got people going through recent disconnects too—people who weren't happy about dates not wanting to meet them."

Luke, Owen, and Jenna walked in before they could throw out any more ideas.

"Okay that's everyone, I think." Catherine stood, addressing the room. "Thank you all for showing up on this short notice and being willing to help."

"We all know you." Cade rolled his eyes as he spoke to his sister. "You can talk normal."

"This is normal, jackass," Catherine threw back at him.

"There's the Catherine we know and love," he tossed back.

"Anyway," she glared at Cade. "I don't need most of you to talk. It will primarily be Evan and Kayla, but I'm going to line everyone up behind them to show support. Jake and Lauren, you'll be in the front. No one is to answer any questions without my approval. Got it?"

Everyone nodded and a few words of agreement were mumbled.

"Great. I have teams working on all the angles we could think of to try to find this liar, but I don't have any success yet. If anyone has any ideas on who or why, please let me know."

"She hired a private investigator," Cade confided to the men.

"That's fucking dangerous." Ryker sat up straighter as he folded his arms across his chest.

"It was that or she do it herself. Besides who knows when it might be good to have a private investigator on the payroll." He shrugged.

"Still dangerous," Ryker muttered.

"Evan, Jake, please join us over here." Catherine motioned for them to come to the table they'd set up for the conference. "People will be showing up within the next half hour, and I want to make sure we're all clear on how to respond."

As he and Jake walked up, Kayla and Lauren were deep in their own conversation and didn't notice them at first.

"How was your date the other night?" Lauren was asking Kayla.

Since when had she had a date? And she hadn't even mentioned it to him? Sure, he'd been a little, or a lot, caught up in his own, but to not even know she had one was unsettling.

"Have a seat here, Evan." Catherine directed him and then moved Jake and Lauren where she wanted them.

The next half-hour passed with Catherine grilling them with questions and then judging their answers. To her credit, each time she stopped them from replying, she would explain why or how it could be misinterpreted.

As they wrapped up and a few reporters showed up, Catherine ushered them away from the table. They always took forever to set up, and then they would all walk in together. It was a part of the plan, in addition to cherry-picking the reporters who got the invitations.

Evan had no right to be as annoyed as he was, and he knew it, but that didn't stop his frustrations from creeping up at finding out that Kayla had been on a date. Why wouldn't she have told him? Was it someone he knew?

The questions flowed through him as he waited for the press conference to start. A few times he almost pulled Kayla to the side but decided against it before they went out there. It was best left for later when their friends were gone and so was the press.

The conference itself lasted a little shy of half an hour. They were able to answer all the questions regarding Blind Date. Most of the reporters were satisfied with the answers, all except the one who ran the original article. He name was John.

John kept pressing the same things regarding background checks and the company they used. Catherine then pressed for his sources to show his story was credible, and that finally stopped him.

It was a quicker process to take everything down and they were easily wrapped up. Catherine was smiling, satisfied with the outcome, and Kayla looked slightly more at ease.

"Can I talk to you for a minute?" Evan whispered to her as their friends chatted.

"What's up?" She faced him.

"In private." He led her to the empty kitchen before facing her again. "Why didn't you tell me you had a date?"

"Wh-what?" Her hair swirled around her as she shook her head.

"I heard you talking to Lauren and she asked about your date." He leaned a hip on the metal counter as he folded his arms and waited for her to respond.

Her eyes widened at first before she returned to her practiced calm demeanor. He knew she didn't want to tell him and couldn't figure out why it bothered him so much.

"Evan, I don't owe you an explanation of my dating life." It came out calm yet forced.

"You don't." He nodded in agreement. "I'm wondering why you wouldn't tell me, though. Is it one of our friends?"

Kayla's jaw actually dropped like something out of a cartoon before she closed her eyes and took a deep breath. "No. And I haven't told you anything because it was a first date and you've been a little preoccupied with yours. However, since you insist on knowing, I didn't go on the date."

"Why not?" he pressed.

"Evan! Drop it."

"Well, where did you meet him? Who is he?"

"Maybe I was going to do my own blind date."

"Maybe? Or really?"

"Does it matter?"

That was the crux of it. Did it matter? For some damn reason, it did. He took too long to reply and watched as Kayla went from annoyed to pissed at him.

"You know what? I'm done. When my friend is done being an asshole, let me know."

She spun and walked out of the kitchen, head high. The click of her heels echoed through the empty kitchen. He was an asshole.

He didn't follow her. He knew better than to chase her down, but he couldn't shake the sense of betrayal that came from her not telling him. It was irrational, but he didn't care anymore. He needed to know.

Chapter Eleven
Kayla

Kayla knocked on Catherine's door, a bottle of wine in each hand. Since meeting Evan, she'd had a chance to hang out with some of the women in his friend group, but she'd never been specifically included in things like a girl's night before.

"You're late," Catherine teased as she opened the door.

"I brought wine though." Kayla held up the bottles.

"Too late for that. Get in here and I'll mix you a drink." Catherine pulled her into the apartment and shut the door.

Catherine's apartment was exactly like something out of a magazine. Jenna and Lauren were in the living room, drinks in hand, waving at her. Nothing about that was odd or unexpected. What was unexpected was the pale pink silk pajamas that everyone was wearing.

"Umm, you guys all match?" Kayla pulled at her own blouse. She was definitely overdressed.

"Yes!" Catherine was giddy. "I got you a pair too. Come on, I'll show you where you can change, and then I'll make your drink."

She followed Catherine down the hall and into a bedroom

where a box waited on the bed with pink tissue paper sticking out. Kayla was having a hard time wrapping her head around these women.

"No one is leaving tonight. We are drinking and gossiping and having fun. You put those on, because I'm going to get you drunk." Catherine was a blur as she closed the door to the bedroom leaving Kayla alone.

Kayla pulled the paper back on the white box and noted the pink silk pajamas waiting for her. Her initials were even on the top. Leave it to Catherine to take it too far.

"Screw it," Kayla laughed. She had good friends here and was going to have a good time.

After slipping the new pajamas on, she looked around for a place to put her clothes, settling on a chair in the far corner. Her phone in hand, she debated leaving it in here with her clothes, but habits were hard to break, and she needed to be available for the restaurant, at least until she was too drunk to be of any help.

Before leaving, she opened the app and sent off a new request to E for a date. The last one had been canceled, but she did want to give it a go, nerves and all. She didn't wait for his reply, heading off in search of her drink.

Catherine thrust it in her hands before she made it all the way down the hall. "Gotta catch up." She winked and took a sip of her own drink.

Kayla took a sip and immediately choked. That was all liquor with a little bit of juice for color. "Oh my God," she managed.

"It's good right?" Catherine left.

They joined everyone on the sofa and one drink turned into several more. A movie played in the background, but they didn't watch any of it.

"So, how are your dates going?" Lauren asked.

Kayla felt her alcohol-flushed face light up with embarrassment. "Shh," she fussed at her friend.

Lauren waved away her concerns. "They all know. Jenna might

not, actually." Lauren turned to face Jenna. "Did you know that Kayla is doing a blind date with Evan?"

"No way! That's so awesome. You guys are such a cute couple," Jenna gushed.

"She was mine and Jake's pick," Lauren said proudly.

"He doesn't know it's me," Kayla reminded her friends.

"Clearly. If he did, you wouldn't be here with us tonight. You'd be at his place doing the nasty." Catherine grabbed a handful of popcorn and shoved it in her mouth.

"Doing the nasty?" Lauren laughed. "How old are you?"

"I'm too young to be this deprived," Catherine muttered.

"If you weren't so hung up on Ryker, then maybe you would date anyone else. Do a blind date of your own, let the app pick." Lauren had somehow called her out and then soothed it over with an idea all in one go.

Kayla stood, wobbled, and sat back down. "He really doesn't know it's me. I need to tell you guys something though."

All three women leaned toward her.

"You can't tell anyone. Not even your significant others."

"I swear," Jenna said.

"Lips are sealed," said Lauren.

"I don't even have anyone to tell," Catherine pouted. "I won't tell anyone, even fictional ones."

Kayla rolled her eyes. Catherine was a wild ride of emotions when she was drinking. She was usually upbeat, but the mood swings tonight were going to give Kayla whiplash.

"He almost kissed me the other night," she confided.

"I thought you hadn't been on a date yet?" Lauren asked.

"No, not the app me, the real me." Kayla pulled her legs up on the sofa beside her, tucking the throw blanket around them. "We haven't. Then he heard you talking to me about my date and got weird."

Lauren threw her head back as she laughed. "Because this is a really good idea."

"Oh, he really likes you," Jenna teased.

"I feel bad about the date though, like I'm lying to him by not telling him it's me when I know it's him," Kayla finally admitted out loud.

"Girl, he is already jealous over your date with him." Catherine tried and failed not to giggle. "That means he's got it bad for you. He'll be excited to find out that it's you."

"What if he's mad?" Kayla asked.

"What if he's not? Just let it roll. It will be a good thing."

Kayla shrugged, she wasn't so sure about that.

"What if we set you up with Ryker?" Lauren asked.

They went back and forth and Kayla took the time to think about what they had said. Was Evan really into her like that? Probably not. He was likely just mad that she hadn't confided in him about her date like he had about his.

Her phone dinged from the couch next to her, and she quickly picked it up, finding a text from Evan.

"Is it him?" Lauren bounced on the sofa.

"You know we are all adults sitting here getting drunk and acting like teenagers, right?" Kayla grinned.

"Yes. Don't care. Is it him?" Lauren demanded.

Kayla nodded.

"Well, don't make us wait. What did he say?" Jenna scooted closer to Lauren who was now almost touching Kayla.

"I haven't opened it yet."

"Wait, which him is it? App him or real him?" Catherine asked.

Kayla rolled her eyes. They were really behaving like kids, but she couldn't deny that she enjoyed it. "Real him." She unlocked her phone and went to her messages. "He's just asking if I'm having a good time."

"He wants to come rescue you," Lauren sang out and clapped her hands together. "You should say no and see what he says."

"I can't do that. Then he will think it's weird when see each other again." It wouldn't work well, but she was curious now if her friends were right.

"Ask him if he was going to kiss you the other day," Catherine suggested.

Kayla's jaw dropped as she faced her friend. "Have you lost your mind?"

Catherine shrugged. "Up for debate for a while now."

"I can't ask him that. It will be weird when I see him again. No."

"You don't have to do anything you don't want to, but I think you should do it," Jenna said in her soothing tone that Kayla was getting used to.

Kayla stared at her phone. "What if he says no?" Her question was quiet, more for herself than anyone else.

"Again, what if he doesn't?" Lauren added.

"You act like you weren't nervous with Jake," Catherine teased. "I seem to recall you panicking when you found out who he was."

"He was literally everything I told you I didn't want." Lauren folded her arm across her chest.

"Oh, stop. It all worked out, and you're so much happier than you were just a few months ago."

A grin spread across Lauren's face. "It did work out well."

"I don't know that I've been thanked yet." Catherine sipped her drink.

"Shut up." Lauren threw a throw pillow at Catherine, hitting her in the face.

As they laughed and joked, Kayla stared at her phone considering her next move. Should she ask him? She wasn't sure at all.

"Shots!" Catherine yelled. "A little liquid courage for our friend here."

She set her phone down and followed everyone to the kitchen.

Lauren stood next to her at the bar. "I'm just giving you a hard time, you know? I wouldn't be at all upset if you didn't text him. I get a little bold when I'm drinking."

Kayla squeezed her friend's hand. "I appreciate it."

Catherine poured them all a shot and lined them up on the bar. "On three, ladies."

Catherine counted up and they all took a shot, everyone coughing after. After everyone recovered, they refilled their drinks and went back to the sofa.

"I'm gonna do it," Kayla announced.

Grabbing her phone, she pulled the message up again.

Kayla: *Were you going to kiss me the other night?*

Immediately the message showed as read, and she tossed it at Lauren. "He read it!" Kayla squealed. "I can't look."

"This is great! Can I look?" Lauren asked, so excited she was bouncing again.

"Go for it." Kayla covered her face as she waited.

"He's typing!" She stood up and faced the sofa. "He keeps stopping and starting again. You know this means the answer is yes."

Catherine and Jenna agreed and jumped up to go look at the phone with Lauren.

"He's calling you!" Lauren handed her the phone.

"What do I do?" Kayla panicked and dropped the phone like it was on fire.

"Answer it!" Catherine encouraged.

"No! This is so embarrassing. I can't talk to him now." Kayla looked at her phone, which had stopped ringing.

"Did he leave a message?" Lauren asked.

Kayla checked but didn't see one. She powered her phone off and shoved it between the cushions of the sofa. "I'm never listening to you guys again," she pouted. "You're bad influences."

"He could have been calling to say yes." Lauren slid next to her and gave her a hug.

"You're such an optimist," Kayla grumbled but couldn't hide her smile.

Chapter Twelve
Kayla

Kayla sat in her office, nursing her hangover and ignoring Evan's calls. She had to get out of her office soon before he showed up for the date she had made yesterday. He had accepted it before she texted him.

Since then, he'd called her a million times. Not one text, only calls. She'd even gotten desperate earlier and texted him and asked what he wanted. He replied with a phone call.

He hadn't really called that much. She shook her head at herself. It was 6 calls throughout the day, which frankly was more patient than she'd be if he had texted her about a kiss. The problem was she didn't know what to say.

She wasn't one to normally get brave when drinking, but she was blaming the fleeting liquid courage on that message. This morning, when she'd woken up on Catherine's sofa with Lauren's feet in her face, she had immediately remembered the message and gotten embarrassed all over again.

She had no idea how she would ever face him again. It was too much to handle and all her own fault.

"He's here!" Her assistant poked her head in Kayla's office.

"Shit." Kayla had sat here too long wallowing and now Evan was here for his date with her and, if she had to guess, he'd be upstairs in her office in a few minutes.

"Stall him," Kayla whispered.

She didn't need to bring anything with her but her purse, so she slipped her heels back on. Instead of heading for the stairs where she might run into him, she went into her private bathroom and shut the door. Her only goal was for him to believe she wasn't around and to go back downstairs.

As she hid, she shook her head at herself. She was in her own bathroom avoiding the man that had become one of her closest friends. She was an idiot—an idiot who wasn't going to go out there and talk to him right now, though.

Muffled voices came through the door. Unable to hear the words, she didn't know if he would be put off or not.

A few minutes later, a soft knocking on the door made her jump.

"He's gone," her assistant said.

Kayla unlocked the door and opened it. "I'm an idiot." She palmed her forehead.

"Knowing is half the battle," she teased. With a wink, she went back to her desk.

"Yeah, yeah." Kayla passed her desk and headed to the restaurant.

Deep breaths, she reminded herself as she waited for the elevator. Evan always used the stairs, so she figured the safest bet was to just wait. By the time it came up and she made it down, Evan would be back in the lobby, waiting to meet his date.

Reaching the ground floor, she went to the other waiting area and checked in with the host. A few people knew she had a date, but all knew not to speak of it. Aside from the nondisclosure agreements she'd made them all sign, she respected her staff and knew that they wouldn't talk.

"Miss K?" a server asked from near the curtain.

Standing, she walked over to him and let him drop the cover of darkness around them.

"Would you like the full experience?" he offered.

A surprised giggle burst forth. "No, thank you. I'm just nervous."

"Most people are when they get here." He took her hand. "My name is Sam, and I'm going to put your hand on my shoulder and lead you to your table. Your date is already waiting."

"Of course he is," she mumbled.

Next time, she was going to have her date wait for her so she could get situated first. Now Evan would be comfortable and her nerves would be overflowing.

"Sam, at the table, please do the whole thing." She didn't want Evan to think she'd been here so many times that she didn't need the instructions.

"You got it."

He led her through the other set of heavy curtains and around the glowing tables. Stopping, he placed her hand on the corner of the table.

"It's a booth. You may slide in here, ma'am," Sam said. As she did, he launched into a well-rehearsed speech on how everything worked.

It was weird, she had to admit. To be here, on a date, in total darkness. People enjoyed the anonymity though, which is why the business model worked so well.

"K?" Evan asked from across the table.

"Hi," she said by way of response.

"It's nice to kind of meet you," he said. "I'd shake your hand, but we'd probably knock something over."

She pictured him winking at the end of that sentence. Evan really flirting was new and different.

"Is there anything to knock over?" she asked.

"Probably not," he admitted.

"I hope you weren't waiting long."

"Not at all. I'm sorry about canceling things on our last date."

"It's okay. I had a work crisis anyway, so I was going to have to do the same. I apologize for taking a while to set up a new one..." She had rehearsed this but suddenly lost the words.

"It's totally fine. I was worried I had upset you, but it seems we were both busy with work."

"That's the way it goes sometimes," she said noncommittally.

Evan cleared his throat. "How have you been? Any more French toast mornings?"

She whisper-laughed. "Can't say there has been that kind of time for me lately."

"That's a shame. Though I won't judge; I've been busy as well."

Their food came and Sam explained how to see everything and so on. The rest of the date passed with small-talk conversations and didn't really touch on anything important.

As they finished their salads, her only hope was that she hadn't disappointed Evan. With his last two dates being completely awful, she didn't want this one to be so mediocre that he wouldn't want to come again.

"It was great to meet you," Evan said. She could hear the smile in his voice.

"You as well." She swallowed the rising worry that he might ask to meet now.

There was a pause before Evan spoke again. "I'm sorry for this. I don't think I'm ready to meet just yet. Nothing is wrong, I promise. I just have a lot going on."

Kayla's body went slack with relief. "No problem. Did you want to try this again, maybe?" she asked hopefully.

"I would love that. Maybe when things calm down at work, we can chat some more in the app?"

Kayla smiled. "I'd love that."

They called Sam over, letting him know they were done, and he prepared to escort Kayla out first. "Thank you for tonight," she told Evan as she stood.

"Thank you for being here."

Evan's sincere voice sent a shiver down her spine.

As she followed Sam, she took note of how heightened her senses really were. Without sight, she could feel everything and her hearing was crazy good too. Everyone spoke at a whisper, but it was like the person was right in your ear.

Sam led her through the curtain. "I'm going to pull the curtain back a bit and let your eyes adjust, and then you'll be good to go."

"Thank you, Sam."

He did and she blinked a few times, letting the light back in slowly. Once adjusted, she walked into the dimly lit lobby that now felt a million times brighter than it ever had.

"Ma'am, you're needed upstairs," the hostess whispered.

Kayla nodded and took the stairs back up to her office. Evan would likely leave after this date since Kayla wasn't there before so she should be fine, or so she told herself.

"What's up?" Kayla asked as she made it upstairs.

"There's something wrong with the scheduling app. I was hoping you could take a look."

Kayla muttered a few swear words as she headed into her office and pulled up the back end of the app to determine the problem. Not seeing anything right away, she looked up to ask what the issue was and locked eyes with Evan.

"Never mind, I was able to fix it," her assistant called before shutting the office door.

"Remind me to give her coal for Christmas," Kayla said to the room, to Evan, to anyone.

"You've been avoiding me," Evan said, staying by the door.

She blew out a breath. "No, I've been busy. What's up?" She avoided his gaze, feeling it on her.

"Kayla," his voice was husky as he said her name.

"What do you need, Evan? I need to head home." She took random shit off her desk and shoved it in her bag to make herself busy.

Standing, she grabbed her now entirely too heavy bag and threw it over her shoulder, preparing to leave. He hadn't replied, but she could feel him still watching her.

"What are you doing?" he asked.

"Leaving."

"With all that?"

"I need it to get some work done this weekend." She had no idea what she'd even grabbed.

He walked over and reached in, pulling something out. "You need your stapler at home to work this weekend?" he questioned.

"Maybe." She was so dumb.

"I think I'm making you nervous, Kayla."

She skirted around him, making for the door. He was spot on but she wasn't going to admit it. With one hand on the door handle, Evan closed in on her, putting his hand on the top of the door.

"Why did you ask me that in your text?"

His breath was close enough to be felt on her neck, and the shiver that rocked through her was unable to be contained.

"Turn around," he commanded.

She wasn't one to listen to a man when he commanded her to do anything, but apparently, that didn't apply to him. Turning to face him was involuntary, a movement she didn't even realize she was doing until it was already done.

Evan lifted her heavy bag off her shoulder and set it on the ground. His hand that wasn't on the door came up to her neck, holding her just below her ear, thumb stroking her cheek, seconds before his lips crashed onto hers.

It wasn't a sweet kiss. It was possessive and hard and hot as hell. His tongue probed for entrance, and she parted her lips, giving it to him. As she did, he groaned, or growled, or some mix of the two, the vibration pulsing through her to her core.

Then, just as quickly as it started, it ended. Evan pulled away, planting one last kiss on her forehead before putting distance between them.

"I hope that answers your question. The next move is yours,

Kayla. I won't hunt you down again. I'll let myself out so you can put all that stuff back on your desk." He held her stapler out for her to take from him.

She took it and stepped away from the door. The second it closed again, she dropped to the floor against it. What the hell was that, and why did she need it again so badly?

Chapter Thirteen
Evan

Today has been shit, Evan thought as he dropped onto this couch. Nothing had gone right at work. He hadn't heard from Kayla either, which was probably the main problem if he was willing to admit that to himself.

Thinking about Kayla brought back more memories of last night and how she was probably never going to talk to him again. He fucked up, but in his defense, she had done it first.

Sure, he'd almost kissed her on her couch that day, but he hadn't. Then she had to go and bring it up like it wasn't already on his mind. Just knowing that a week later it was on her mind still too had been all it took.

It hadn't been his intention to kiss her when he went to her office. He wanted to talk to her. Then she'd been so nervous and packed half her desk into her bag that he couldn't help it. Never in his life had he seen Kayla nervous, and it just did something to him.

He had taken charge, and sweet God, she'd let him. Then he'd kissed her and walked away. Had he stayed, it would have been more than kissing, and he wasn't so far gone that he didn't recognize that they both needed space to process that kiss.

Hot was an understatement. It had rocked his world in a way that no other kiss had. It was electric, and he wanted more. Hopefully, she did too. Now he just had to hope that she would reach out, because he wasn't sure he could handle it if she didn't.

Around lunchtime, he'd gotten another message from K in the app. He hadn't opened it yet and wasn't sure he wanted to until he heard from Kayla.

Something about her at the restaurant had been off, and he couldn't place a finger on what it was. It could have just been nerves, for his part, but she seemed familiar. Leave it to his friends to set him up with someone he already knew.

Ignoring the message, Evan scrolled through his contacts to see who he knew that started with K, other than Kayla. A few names stood out, but they were all easily dismissed just by what he knew of her from chatting and voice alone.

They whispered in the restaurant, but he was positive that at least one K in his phone didn't know how to whisper. She was louder than everyone in the room, always. Thank God it wasn't her.

Giving in, he opened K's message and read it.

K: *Thank you for dinner. I had a good time meeting you.*

E: *I did too.*

He didn't elaborate or try to start a conversation on purpose. He needed to figure out what the hell he wanted before he did. It felt wrong to talk to K after going up and kissing Kayla last night. It felt even more wrong that he had gone and kissed Kayla after a date with someone else.

He was screwing everything up and he knew it. He didn't know how to stop though. Kissing Kayla wasn't something he would regret, now or ever. Unless she stopped talking to him because of it, then he'd regret it.

That was the reason he hadn't kissed her last weekend. He didn't want to screw up their friendship, and look at him now—completely screwed. He was dating one woman and kissing another.

After thinking about it for a few minutes with no sudden realization of what to do, he stood and went to his fridge to get some dinner. Too many K's, and he had no idea what to do about it.

Determined not to think of either one of them, he pulled out some leftover chicken and got to work making himself a plate. It didn't take long to warm up; he carried it to the bar and ate.

Not taking nearly as much time as he wanted, he looked around for anything else to do. Normally he'd call and talk to Kayla, but that was out of the question, which only brought his mind back to her.

His phone rang, and he snatched it up hoping it was her. Instead, Jake's name appeared on the screen.

"Hey," he answered.

"I heard a story about you," Jake teased.

Evan paled. "What?" It wasn't that he didn't want anyone to know, but what if she'd complained?

"Apparently when all the girls hung out this weekend, Kayla told everyone that she thought you were going to kiss her."

Evan blew out a breath. "Yeah, I know."

"Did you?"

"Yes."

"Why didn't you then?" Jake asked.

"Because it's Kayla."

"So? You want Kayla, and you guys already act like you're in a relationship anyway."

"What's that supposed to mean?"

Jake laughed. "Nothing bad. You're always together, she's your best friend in everything. Hell, she's even been your plus-one to the charity thing."

Evan thought about it; she had. He hadn't even considered trying to find a date; she was the first one he'd asked. "I don't know if it would work."

"Why? You guys have chemistry. And to hear Lauren talk about it, she wanted you to kiss her, man."

"I did something." Evan's voice was quiet.

"What?"

"You can't tell anyone and that includes Lauren. But she might already know." She probably did.

There was rustling. Jake was clearly moving around.

"You okay?" Jake asked.

"I don't know."

"What is going on? I won't tell anyone." Concern was clear in Jake's voice.

"I went on my date yesterday."

"Is that it? Was it that bad again?"

"No. I think I know this person in real life, but I don't know who it is."

Jake laughed. "Okay and?"

"Then I went upstairs to talk to Kayla because she texted me and asked if I had almost kissed her when they were all hanging out. She'd been avoiding me and my calls since that text. I'm pretty sure she turned her phone off right after sending it."

"She did," Jake confirmed.

"How do you—Lauren. Never mind that. I went to her office after my date, and she was there so I confronted her."

"How'd that go?"

"She panicked and started packing everything on her desk, refusing to look at me. Then I held the door closed and kissed her."

"Woah. What did she say?"

"Not a damn thing. I was kind of pissed off still, so I left and told her I hoped that it answered her question and I wasn't going to chase her. She'd have to call me."

Jake blew out a breath. "Damn."

"I haven't heard from her. What if I fucked it all up?"

"Give her time. I'm sure you'll hear from her soon."

"I'm not sure."

"Look, she'll take a bit to process and then reach out to you. I promise if I hear anything from Lauren, I will let you know which way things are leaning. She wanted to kiss you, that I do know."

"Maybe."

"It was just last night. Give it time. Maybe she's working."

"The restaurant is closed on Mondays."

"Still, she works as much as you."

It was true. She was probably working on something. He should do the same and take his mind off her for a bit.

"How'd the date go?" Jake asked.

"It was okay. Nothing to write home about, but I plan to see her again, unless Kayla wants to, I don't know." His phone beeped, another call coming in. "She's calling me." Evan stared at it in shock.

"Answer it!" Jake's laughter was cut off by the call ending.

He cleared his throat before answering. "Hi."

"Evan—" Her voice was shaky.

His muscles tensed immediately, something was wrong. "What's going on?"

"The restaurant. I was upstairs, and I heard glass and it's a mess, and I don't know..."

"Kayla, did you call the police?" Evan asked, already slipping his shoes on. "I'm on my way there."

"I called them. They told me to lock myself in my office while I waited for them. I did that."

"Just hang tight. I'll be there shortly."

Silence met him.

"Are you there?" he asked.

"I'm scared, Evan." She was crying, he'd bet on it.

"Stay on the phone with me then, okay? I'm going to my car now and I'll be there." Again, nothing was said. "Kayla, talk to me baby so I know you're there."

"I don't like being scared," she admitted.

"I don't like you being scared either." Why hadn't the dispatcher stayed on with her while the police came? Wasn't that what they were supposed to do? It's what they did in police shows anyway, but that was fiction.

Evan flew through the city with Kayla's soft crying coming out of the speakers of his car. One thing he knew for sure, when he found out who did this, he was going to hunt them down for making Kayla this scared.

"I'm just around the corner, okay?"

"Mm-hmm."

Red and blue lights flashed as he pulled up. "The police are here, baby. I'll come get you, okay?"

She sniffed and he hoped she'd heard him.

Chapter Fourteen
Evan

Evan had come and gotten her from her office as promised. He hadn't left her side since. Kayla was torn between being comforted and feeling smothered.

Throughout the police questioning her, Evan had sat with her, his hand wrapped around hers the whole time. He hadn't mentioned last night, and for that she was grateful.

She still hadn't been out to see any of the damage. The only thing she knew was what she had seen when she ran down there, but it was a blink before she ran back up the stairs terrified. Then she'd called the police and then Evan.

"Miss, we are going to need to see that footage now," an officer said to her.

She nodded. "I can pull it up in my office."

Kayla stood and Evan came with her. She led them into her office and unlocked her computer, going to the security system. It was another few clicks to pull up the time and then she hit play.

They all watched as two men threw bricks through the restaurant's windows. That was the sound she heard. They came inside after the windows broke.

"Wait," Evan said. "Let me."

He flipped back a few frames and paused it. There, leaning up against a car right outside the front door was a familiar face—Lauren's mother.

"Why?" Kayla said shocked.

Evan chatted with the officer while she stared at the screen. She'd caused problems once already, but she was pretty sure Jake had paid the woman off. Plus, Jake and Lauren were living together, so what was her point here?

"We need to flip to the other camera now, okay?" Evan's soothing voice washed over her. "I'll do it."

He took over, and she watched as the video showed the two men coming in and ransacking the lobby before going behind the curtains and yanking them down. At one point, she saw herself running down the stairs and then right back up them, terrified.

Evan moved to the other camera, and she watched the true damage unfold. In a matter of minutes, there was so much damage.

They wouldn't be able to open tomorrow at all. A pit settled in her stomach. They weren't going to be able to open for a while; it was a crime scene.

Without realizing it, her breathing had picked up, her heart racing along with it. Evan squeezed her shoulder and crouched down to see her face as she sat in the chair.

"It's going to be okay. Take a deep breath," he soothed.

She didn't want to take a deep breath. She wanted to rage, to scream and fight, and then she'd go pull up her pants and deal with it. Instead, she did as Evan suggested and tried to even out her breathing. Freaking out wasn't going to solve anything.

When she brought her focus back to the room, she realized they were alone. "Where'd he go?"

"I sent him all the videos already. There's nothing else he needs up here. Look at me," he pleaded.

She did, but all that did was make her want to cry again. Evan pulled her up and into his arms.

"It's okay," he repeated as she cried in his arms.

It felt good, safe, to be held by him and she decided not to question it tonight. She needed strength, and he was offering his, so she'd take it.

"I need to call Jake," he whispered into her hair.

Kayla nodded against his chest as he reached for his phone. When she tried to pull away, he tightened his other arm around her, keeping her close.

He spoke to Jake for a minute before hanging up. "They are on their way. He needs to see this."

"Lauren is coming?" she asked, stepping out of his hold.

"Yes. I don't know how this is going to go. If you want, I can show them. You don't have to be in here when I do."

"I want to be here. It's not her fault."

"It's not." He looked her over. "Are you okay?"

Kayla nodded again. "I think so. It scared me to death."

"Me too. I was so worried." He pulled her in for another hug, and she went willingly, her arms wrapping around him. "God, I'm so glad you weren't hurt."

"Thank you for coming," she told him.

He pulled back, holding her an arm's length away. "Don't you ever doubt for a second that I won't come for you. Anytime, day or night, got it?"

She didn't have any words. The tears started again, and she tried to wipe them away, but they kept coming.

"Baby, please don't cry," Evan pleaded with her.

A watery laugh slipped through. "All this and it's my tears that rattle you?"

"I don't want to see you upset, Kayla." His voice was firm, there was no doubting that he meant it.

"I need to see it," she told him.

Evan blew out a resigned sigh. "Come on."

He held her hand and led her downstairs and into the restaurant. She took in the overturned chairs and tables. Glass was everywhere from all the drinking glasses they had tossed around. Red spray paint covered every surface in some way.

"How did they do all this?" she turned to him. "Why, Evan?"

"We're going to figure it out," he promised.

"What the hell?" came Jake's voice from the lobby.

"In here," Evan called.

All his friends poured in. Even Luke had come, and she knew him less than Ryker because he had rarely shown up to things lately.

"What the fuck happened?" Ryker said, crunching glass as he walked in.

"Let's go upstairs," Kayla told Evan.

"Yeah. We don't need everyone in here like this." He turned to his friends. "Upstairs."

One by one, they turned and headed for the side door that led to the stairwell. She and Evan brought up the rear.

"How did they all get here so fast?" she asked.

Evan shrugged. "I don't underestimate any of us when one is in trouble."

When they reached the top of the stairs, Lauren pulled her away from Evan. "What happened? Are you okay? Who did this?" Her questions came rapid fire.

"Can you just turn my monitor around, Evan? So everyone can see?" Kayla asked.

She stood, holding her friend as Evan just hit play. Everyone focused on the two men on the screen, and she knew the moment that Lauren recognized her mother on the screen.

Her whole body stiffened with her sharp intake of breath. "Why?" she whispered.

Jake came over and Lauren sank into his arms. "It's not your fault."

"It isn't," Kayla agreed.

"But it's my mother. I'm so sorry. I don't know what she wants."

"Probably more money." Jake's voice was harder than she'd ever heard it.

Evan made his way around his friends and was one again touching her. Kayla tried to step away since all his friends were watching, but he wasn't having it.

She sighed; it wasn't worth an argument in front of everyone. She'd talk to him later about it.

Cade was the first one to spring into action. "I'm calling Catherine."

Ryker was next. "Call your insurance now so we can start cleaning up. We need to take pictures."

"I've got my camera in the car." Luke jumped up and headed out.

"I have some calls to make, too," Jake said.

"We need to help." Lauren stood and looked at Kayla. "I'm so sorry."

Kayla went to her friend and squeezed her hand. "It's not your fault."

"Can't help it," she shrugged. "What can I do?"

"I—" she looked at Evan. She genuinely didn't know what to do.

"Can you keep Kayla company while she calls the insurance and wait for Catherine? I don't want anyone alone until we know what's going on."

"Yep!" Lauren held up their linked hands.

"Lock this." Jake kissed Lauren before he walked out the office door.

Evan was on his heels and then she heard him. "Fuck it." He turned around and pulled Kayla in for a quick kiss before leaving and closing the door.

Lauren went over and locked it before throwing a questioning glance back at Kayla. "That needs an explanation. Maybe not right now, but I need details."

Still shocked, she stared at the door. "As soon as I know what they are, I'll let you know."

"Fair." Lauren fixed her computer to face the right direction. "Who do we need to call?"

The call to the insurance company was short. Most of the details were in the videos that she was able to supply them, and somewhere downstairs pictures were being taken. Catherine came in, shocked, just as she was wrapping up the call.

"What the hell happened?" she said. "I mean, obviously I can see, but what the hell?"

"My mother," Lauren confessed.

"That bitch again?" She dropped into one of the chairs. "Fuck her. Not your fault."

"I keep telling her that," Kayla added.

"See?" Catherine added.

"Just give me a minute to process it all. I'll be okay. This is about Kayla and not me, though."

Catherine studied her for a minute and then went back to Kayla. "Okay, you've got your favorite PR rep. Let's do damage control."

Time passed as Catherine quickly decided on a plan and started getting information out on social media. She sent a copy of what to put in her emails to guests, and Kayla got that sent out, canceling reservations for the week and processing refunds.

Lauren monitored both phones for messages from the men downstairs and Kayla's incoming emails. Together, they had done all the damage control they could for one night.

The men appeared not long after they finished. All five men were towering in her office, but she only had eyes for one. Damn her foolish heart.

"I'll take you home," Evan said, approaching her.

"My car is here," Kayla reminded him.

"Mine's not. Anyone going my way?" Catherine asked the room.

"I am," Ryker said.

Kayla met Lauren's shocked expression. Ryker usually did his best to avoid Catherine, damn sure not offering her a ride when there were a ton of other people here that could do it.

"We can come back for it," Evan said.

Distracted for the first time all night, she nodded. She'd figure her car thing out tomorrow. What she needed right now were more details on the development with Ryker and Catherine.

"Ryker has a few construction buddies; they patched the windows up, so we can leave anytime," Evan said.

"I've got security coming to guard so nothing else happens," Cade added.

"You don't have to do that," she said.

Cade faced her. "You know you're one of our group, right? This is what we do for each other, whatever we can."

Cade turned and left her office, with everyone else filing out after him, leaving her and Evan alone.

"What do you need?" Evan asked.

"Just my purse. Nothing else is important."

"Got it."

She laughed at her purse strung over his shoulder. He held out his hand and she took it, letting him lead her from the room and the disaster that awaited her tomorrow.

Chapter Fifteen
Kayla

As they pulled up to her apartment, Kayla was itching to get out of the car. She yanked the door open as soon as he stopped.

"Wait!" Evan yelled. "Let me walk you up."

"It's okay. Thank you for coming. I think I can get to my apartment by myself." She just needed to get away from him before all these feelings about him overwhelmed her. It was getting more and more challenging to find the line between friends or something more.

"Kayla, please."

She hesitated. That did her in, and he caught up to her.

"We don't know why she targeted the restaurant or if she's decided that she has something against you specifically. I'm just worried about you."

What was she supposed to say to that? That was part of the problem, though. As long as he kept saying things like that, calling her baby, and kissing her, she couldn't keep her distance. If she didn't, then she ran a real risk of losing her friend, and that was more important to her than anything else.

They didn't speak as they rode the elevator up. Kayla's thoughts were all over the place. She wanted him, there was no denying it. But at what cost? Evan was an amazing guy, and she couldn't imagine her life without him in it anymore.

The elevator dinged and they stepped out. It was a quick walk down the hall to her door.

"Thank you for letting me walk you up," Evan said at her door. "I know I'm being a bit much. Today scared the hell out of me."

"Do you want to come in for a minute?" Apparently, her mouth was making decisions without her brain's input.

She just opened the door and Evan followed. There was no doubt that he would. The question was, what happens now?

"Kayla, I need you to promise me something."

"What?" she said wearily.

He stepped forward and cupped her cheek as he held her gaze. "Never run into danger again. I think I lost ten years of my life today."

"I didn't do it on purpose. I was checking out the noise."

Somehow his gaze was even more tender than before. "You have cameras. I just need to know you're safe."

"If it helps, I don't intend to do it again."

"That helps, a lot."

She reached up and touched his hand, leaning into it. "Really, thank you for being there for me today."

"Always."

She pushed all thoughts away from her mind and went only on instinct. Leaning forward, she pressed her lips to his.

Evan froze for a moment before he pulled her closer, her body melding into his. He deepened the kiss, his tongue exploring, dancing with hers. It was different than their last kiss. There was no rush.

Kayla let her hands roam over him. Bold now with his reaction, she wanted more. Her hands ran through his hair, her nails scratching his scalp as he moaned.

Evan pulled back a fraction, and she opened her eyes in question. "Kayla, I have to go or I won't want to stop."

"I didn't ask you to." Kayla closed the gap again, pressing her lips to his.

"Are you sure?" he asked.

She backed away with a sigh, linking her hand in his. Instead of words, she'd show him that she was sure. He went willingly with her down the hall and into her bedroom.

Reaching the bed, Kayla turned and faced Evan again. His eyes were dark, and it turned her on even more than she already was. His look made her feel powerful and desired.

Kayla sat on the bed and scooted backward, looking up at Evan and arching a brow. "This is what I want as long as you want it too."

He backed away, and she thought he was going to leave. If he did, she'd die of embarrassment.

It was only a step back though and his eyes roamed her body. "Take off your top and skirt," he ordered.

Without thought, she scrambled out of them and laid back down again. Her red lace bra and matching thong had been put on with thoughts of him this morning, never expecting him to see them. Now he was looking at her like he was ready to tear them off.

He climbed onto the bed, his hands sliding from her thighs upward and over her hips until they reached her breasts. "You are so fucking beautiful," he said.

Evan's lips covered hers, his hands cupping her breasts over her bra as he kissed her. She loved her breasts getting his attention, and Evan must have realized her excitement because he brought his knee up between her legs, putting pressure where she needed it.

"You like that." It wasn't a question; it was a fact. He was calling it out like he was learning something new and committing it to memory. "What about this?"

He kissed a path from her lips down her neck, finding her bra strap with his hands and sliding them down as he kissed a path of exposed flesh. She moaned, the anticipation building in her.

Finally, he freed her breasts, and his hands went back to touching. He palmed her breasts, then pressed them up from the bottom and took both nipples between his finger and thumb. A light squeeze and twist and she cried out.

"I'm going to say you like that, too."

Bending down, he took one pert nipple in his mouth and sucked. She lifted off the bed. Then he bit down, just enough to feel a little pain with the pleasure.

"Evan," she half-yelled.

"I'm going to learn every inch of you tonight. I want to see you come over and over."

She was riding the edge as it was and didn't respond.

"What else do you like?" he asked.

She whimpered in response as his knee released its pressure on her, leaving her wanting.

"I'll take care of you," he assured her.

He continued kissing his path down her body, and she tensed as he reached her panty line. His hands toyed with the waist of them before pulling them down her legs. She lost his weight on her as he pulled away to peel them off.

"I have imagined doing this to you so many times. I want to know your taste. Can I do that?"

"Mm-hmm," she answered.

He didn't speak again. Instead, he slid his hands under her knees, drawing her legs apart. Draping one knee over his shoulder, he let his hand lead the way, slipping one finger into her.

She hissed a breath as every nerve ending in her body pulsed with his touch. He added a second finger and pumped them in and out of her a few times.

Just when she thought this was too much, already building towards her orgasm, Evan bent down and flattened his tongue against her clit. She cried out, pulling up off the bed at the sheer pleasure of it.

As she worked towards her orgasm, Evan continued to use his fingers and tongue to guide her over the edge. Suddenly, he pulled his fingers out of her before adding a third, stretching her in the best way possible. Then he sucked once on her clit, and she saw stars.

She came with an unbelievable force. Crying out his name, she clutched the quilt under her as he continued his ministrations and guided her back down from that earth-shattering orgasm.

"I knew you would taste like heaven," he said as he pulled away from her, drawing his shirt over his head.

Kayla licked her lips in anticipation as she watched this perfect man strip in front of her. She needed more, needed to feel him deep inside of her. His pants fell to the ground, his hard cock stretching against his boxers.

He slid those off next and took one hand to stroke his cock a few times as he looked at her. "Seeing you there, waiting and ready for me, is the hottest thing I've ever seen." He bent down, grabbed his wallet, and pulled out one foil packet. He tore it open and rolled it over himself.

Evan grabbed her legs again, surprising her by pulling her to the edge of the bed. Her tall bed made it the perfect angle for him to stand and slide into her, which is exactly what he did before pulling all the way out and then thrusting in again in one move.

Kayla closed her eyes as she enjoyed the way he felt. Surprisingly, she felt another orgasm building. She'd never had two in one session. Hell, often she didn't have one.

Standing, Evan continued his forceful thrusts over and over into her. Unable to touch him from this position, she gripped the quilt again as she cried out to Evan's movements. Her head tossed side to side as she searched for anything to push her over.

"Tell me what you need," Evan said.

She shook her head, nowhere near about to tell him what she wanted. Kayla had a secret that she was holding on to, and she'd rather miss out than tell him.

"Say it," Evan commanded.

Eyes closed, she refused.

"Dammit. I'm too far gone already. Next time I'll have you say it," Evan ground out as he pumped into her still.

Then he did the thing she needed. A little pain with her pleasure, one hand dropped to her nipple and gave it another pinch and twist.

That was it. She flew over the edge and rode high on the waves of her second orgasm, barely registering how loud she was being as Evan pulsed inside of her, finding his own release. It took them both a minute to ease back down from their highs.

Evan panted as he pulled out of her. "You fucking undo me." Bending down, he kissed her before pulling away and disappearing into the bathroom.

Kayla didn't move, or more accurately, couldn't move. Her limbs were like Jell-O, and she was too sated to care that she was still lying there naked a few seconds later when he returned from disposing of the condom.

He pulled the blanket down and scooped her into his arms, placing her on a pillow and pulling the covers up over her.

"Stay," she heard herself beg.

"Just going to the other side of the bed," Evan chuckled.

True to his word, he climbed in beside her and wrapped one arm over her waist. She relaxed even further as Evan pressed another kiss into her hair.

Chapter Sixteen
Evan

Evan rolled over in the bed, finding it cold and empty. She'd left him here in her bed, and he immediately felt the stinging pain of loss.

He stood and hunted down his boxers and pants, slipping them on before going in search of her. There was no chance of a repeat unless she had a stash of condoms somewhere, which for some reason, he doubted. But he wanted to find her, be near her again.

She was in the kitchen, cooking if his nose wasn't lying to him. Turning the corner, he spotted her, already up and dressed and cooking.

Coming up behind her, he kissed the top of her head as he pulled her in for a quick hug. "Good morning."

Kayla jumped, squealed, and the spatula in her hand went flying. "You scared me!" She fussed, pulling away from him and picking the spatula up off the floor.

"That was definitely not my intent." He took the spatula from her and carried it over to the sink to wash it. "I'll finish your eggs. I didn't mean to scare you."

He should have thought about that, especially after last night. It hadn't even been a whole day since that happened. Of course, she would be jumpy.

"I'll finish them. You go sit down." Kayla waved him off.

Still shirtless, Evan took a seat at the bar and watched her. Hopefully, she didn't have plans today and he could run to the store and then spend the day with her. Work would wait; he didn't have anything pressing that needed to be done today.

Kayla pulled two plates down and piled eggs on each before opening the oven and pulling out bacon. Then she turned and placed one in front of him before turning back for a fork.

"Enjoy," she said.

She kept her gaze down, focused on her plate. It was quiet as they ate, and he could feel the tension building.

"About last night," she started.

"Don't regret it," Evan pleaded.

"I'm not sure we should do that again." Kayla said quietly, not looking up at him.

"What?" Evan choked out. "Why?" Then a thought popped in his head. "Was I too much? I mean, I thought you were into it, but I don't have to—"

Kayla finally looked up at him. "No. You weren't, I mean it wasn't. Ugh. There was nothing wrong with it."

"Then what's the problem?"

"What if we ruin this?" She gestured between them.

He sighed. At least he fully understood where she was coming from, but after last night, he wasn't going to let her go that easily. He'd fight for her. "We won't. Last night was more than I could have imagined. If you need time to process it, I'll stand behind you for as long as you need. Don't regret it."

"I don't regret it," she said.

"Then think about it instead of deciding right now that it can never happen again, please? That's all I'm asking from you. I'll give you space about it, but don't shut it down, please?" He was on the verge of begging and didn't like it, but he hoped she'd listen to him and at least think about it.

Her shoulders fell, and he felt like an asshole.

"Okay," she answered.

"I'll just get out of your hair then."

He put his plate in the sink and went back to her bedroom, looking for his shirt. This wasn't at all what he had expected after last night. Disappointed, he picked his shirt up off the floor and slipped it back on.

Not that he blamed her. Hadn't that been his exact fear of even kissing her?

Walking past her still at the bar, he slipped his shoes on and headed for the door. There was no point in staying, and he couldn't even kiss her goodbye.

"Let me know if you hear from the police or the insurance?" he asked.

"I will."

"I won't bring this up about us again while we deal with the restaurant. I don't want you to feel like you can't call me."

She nodded. "Will you let me know if you hear from Jake?"

"You'll be the first to know."

He opened the door and headed down the hall. What a fucking roller coaster of emotions these last few hours had been. He'd respect her need for space as long as he could.

He would ask for time, ask her to think it through, but he'd never push her too hard. If she gave it thought and decided she didn't want to be with him, well, that would fucking suck, but he'd accept it.

The worst part wasn't her second thoughts though. Or even those thoughts mirroring his own. No, it was the fact that he was pretty sure they'd already ruined their friendship.

He went home, showered, and went to work, hoping for a distraction from his thoughts. It was short-lived as every thought came back to Kayla. Everyone had heard about the restaurant by now, and it seemed every single person in his office stopped by to talk about it.

Jake called to say they were looking for Lauren's mom, her name lost somewhere in the conversation. Not that it mattered what it was. All that mattered was the damage she had done, probably in some misguided attempt to get money out of them.

His phone was full of texts from everyone asking how he was doing and if there were any updates. The one person he wanted to hear from was keeping him in the dark.

It was late in the afternoon when Kayla finally called. He had to take a few breaths before answering as excitement built at seeing her name on the screen even though he knew it was likely she was calling about the restaurant.

"Hey," Evan answered.

"I heard from the insurance company."

He resisted the urge to swear. He knew she must be calling about business, but it still hurt to know that for sure. "What did they say?"

"He's already been out to the restaurant. I didn't know or I would have been there."

"Why didn't they call us?" They should have.

"They did. I fell asleep and didn't hear it. The security people called Cade and got permission to let him in when I didn't answer."

"I'm sorry. Did you get some good sleep at least?"

She made a non-committal noise. "They said it will be more than a month before we can even start thinking about re-opening."

That caught his attention, and he jerked upright in his chair. "A month?"

"It's going to take time to get all the bids in and then to get the supplies and get it done." She sounded so defeated.

"We'll come up with something in the meantime," Evan told her.

"I don't want to think about it right now. I'll deal with it tomorrow and call Catherine."

"Let me know if I can help with anything."

"Okay."

"Kayla, I'm serious. Everything else aside, I'm invested in the restaurant, too. I want things to work out for you and for it." He was quite literally an investor.

"I know. I just need to process all of this. Maybe wallow in some self-pity with a gallon of ice cream and then I'll be back to normal. For now, all the guests for this week are taken care of. We did it last night, so I don't need to do anything right now."

"Do you want me to call Catherine?" he offered.

"Please don't. I love her, but I don't want a bunch of people showing up over here tonight."

"Understood. Promise you'll call if you need anything or want to talk?"

"Sure."

The call ended and Evan felt worse than he had this morning. This wasn't good news. At least he had something to do now. He had to figure out how to help this process move faster.

Chapter Seventeen
Kayla

Kayla woke early Wednesday morning, surprised she'd slept at all. Between Evan and the restaurant, she was worn out but couldn't stop thinking about them.

Yesterday after Evan had left, she had decided that she wasn't doing anything. She didn't talk to hardly anyone and only barely functioned, and then she'd fallen asleep and had missed the insurance company's first call.

She was sore, too, which was making it hard to get Evan off her mind. She almost didn't want to. Then she remembered that she'd gotten exactly what she wanted, and it couldn't have come at a worse time in her life.

Evan would be there for her no matter what, she knew this without hesitation, but was she in the right mind to be making decisions like this, ones that would impact everything in her life going forward? Had she already ruined it by inviting him in last night? Probably.

That was the hardest thing to accept. She wanted Evan here, helping her deal with everything, but at the same time, she needed space. This was why friends shouldn't turn into lovers, no matter how hot they are or how incredibly good the sex was.

It had been good, too. Never had she had two orgasms in one session, much less in one night. He'd also been surprisingly commanding, something she didn't know she liked. He had thrown in just the right amount of what she needed—she was getting excited again thinking about it.

Pushing those thoughts aside, she headed out of her apartment. She needed to go and look at the damage with fresh eyes and then start making calls and plans.

With a new resolve, she held her head high as she left. She needed to handle business. No more wallowing in the nonsense. It was time to deal with it.

Security guards stood blocking the plywood-covered door as she pulled up to the restaurant. The driver of the rideshare let her out right in front, and she thanked him before heading off. Her car was still in the parking garage from two nights ago when Evan had driven her home.

He must have forgotten because there was no way that he would have left it there. She was grateful he did, though. It was better than driving herself, and it gave her a deadline to get out of the house by.

"Hi, gentleman," she said to the two men.

One of them opened the door for her. "We haven't had any trouble."

"Thank you," Kayla answered as she stepped through, surprised there was no glass on the ground anymore.

They didn't report to her, or maybe they did. She wasn't really sure, but she was glad to hear that nothing more had happened. Not that it would really matter at this point considering all the damage that had already been done.

Someone had swept up most of the glass, she noted. It wasn't just gone from the entryway but pretty much everywhere. Looking around the dining room, she noticed that some other things had been cleared as well.

Maybe the insurance had started work on that part already. She shrugged and went up to her office. A quick call to Catherine confirmed that she would come by today to work on their next steps.

"Kayla?" Lauren's voice echoed up the stairs.

Sighing, she went to the stairs and called back down. "I'm up here." She waited until her friend reached the top of the stairs before going back to her office.

Lauren followed. "I'm so sorry about everything. I'll help pay for whatever needs to be done."

Kayla turned to face her. "You will not. That's what insurance is for. And stop apologizing; you didn't do this."

"I know." Lauren took a seat. "I tried calling you yesterday."

"I just needed some time to process everything."

"Understandable. What can I help with? Give me anything, something, to do."

Kayla looked over at her friend who was no doubt having her own inner turmoil. "I'm mostly waiting on Catherine and trying to pull the number of refunds and dates to cancel."

"Cancel more? Did you hear from the insurance company?"

"They said a month at least."

Lauren scoffed. "That's ridiculous. Between any of the guys, they can get something moving much faster. I mean other than the glass, a lot of it is just clean up and ordering new stuff, right?"

"I don't know. The adjuster sent over a report, but I don't know what half this shit means."

"Something for me to do, then. Email it to me, and I'll see if I can make heads or tails of it."

Kayla did and they both sat there quietly working on their own stuff for a while until Catherine interrupted them.

"It looks better than it did Monday night down there," she commented as she walked in.

Kayla looked up from her computer to greet Catherine. "I don't know who cleaned it up. I wasn't here yesterday."

"Your guards might have done it."

"Not my guards; they're your brother's," Kayla reminded her.

"They are yours while they are here. Why do you sound pissed off about it?"

"Hey," Lauren interrupted. "Why don't we order some lunch and you can tell us about your ride home with Ryker while we wait, and then we can get started?"

"I guess," Catherine answered.

Kayla nodded and Lauren ordered something.

"Hate to ruin your need for a good story, but he drove me home, I got out, the end," Catherine said.

"It's a big deal that he offered, though?" she asked.

"It was definitely out of character for him, and I thought he wanted to say something, but he never did." Catherine got comfortable and set up her laptop.

Kayla didn't comment. She had thoughts, but she didn't want to tell anyone her own stuff until she had sorted that out, and she wasn't sure she was in a good headspace to give anyone else advice.

"Wonder what it was?" Lauren asked.

"I didn't push him. He avoids me at all costs, always. It was weird enough for him to offer to drive me home, so I didn't question anything else. I'm trying to put that man out of my mind."

Kayla snorted.

"You're one to talk," Catherine said.

"I didn't say anything," Kayla replied.

"Please don't, you guys," Lauren intervened again. "We are all tense over the vandalism. No need for us to fight."

"I'm sorry. I'm being a bitch. It's not on purpose," Kayla apologized to her friends. "Can we make a plan? I think I just need to go and stop thinking about this."

Catherine stood and walked over to Kayla behind her desk. "Babe, what is going on?" She bent down and gave her a hug.

That was all it took. She didn't want sympathy or anything from them because she'd start crying again. And she did. Lauren joined the group hug, and they both murmured to her how it was all going to be okay.

"It's a lot," Kayla admitted as they pulled away. "They said it was going to be a month or more."

"Have Evan hire someone else," Catherine said.

"No, I'm just going to let the insurance handle it."

"Why?" Catherine's shock was mirrored in Lauren's expression.

"I don't need him to come in and save everything." Saying it out loud sounded stupid, like a teenager refusing to do something because she was asked.

"What happened with you two?" Lauren asked. "He's your friend. Plus, isn't he your partner here?"

"I don't want him to." That was the whole answer. If he did then she'd see him more and then she'd fall into bed with him again.

Her phone rang, cutting off their conversation. She'd never been more grateful for a distraction.

"Hello?" she answered the unknown number.

"Hi, is this the owner of Blind Date?" a man's voice said.

"It is," she confirmed. "I'm not currently doing interviews, though, sorry."

"I'm calling from Milestone Construction about the work needed. We were contracted today and requested to start as soon as possible."

"By the insurance company?" Confused, she looked around for a pen to take their information. "They said it would take a while to get started."

"No ma'am. We were contracted directly from a Mr. Evan—"

Kayla cut him off. "What?" She stood, pissed.

"I just wanted to touch base with you and see when we could meet and get started," the man said, skipping over her outburst.

"I'm going to have to call you back."

Kayla ended the call and grabbed her keys. "I'm going to hurt him. Evan hired a contractor to start immediately."

"That's good news," Catherine reminded her.

"I want to do this on my own! Why does no one see that?" Kayla raged.

She stormed out, leaving her friends staring after her. To their credit, they didn't follow but they'd probably call Evan and warn him. No matter, he was still going to get what was coming to him.

Chapter Eighteen
Evan

Evan sat in his office at work, finally content that he had done something to help Kayla move on from what had happened. Maybe if she wasn't focused on that, she'd realize that things weren't all bad.

He'd called in a few favors, paid a deposit, and then gave them Kayla's number. Now all she had to do was pick out what needed to be replaced, let them work, and watch as it happened. With any luck, their timeframe would be much shorter than the insurance company's.

His phone rang and he answered it. Jake hopefully had an update on Lauren's mother.

"No news. We've been trying to track her down but it's proving difficult," Jake told him.

"How can that be?"

"She's hiding and apparently pretty good at it. If she's staying at any nearby hotels, she's not under her name."

"Could someone be behind her?" It wouldn't even be that surprising.

"Looking into it. It's more likely that she's working alone, but you never know."

"Not with her."

"Agreed."

Jake cleared his throat. "That's not why I called, though."

"What's up? Everything okay?"

"Honestly, not sure. Lauren called and said Kayla left her office in a rage threatening to harm you," Jake told him.

"Why?" He racked his brain, trying to figure out what he possibly could have done.

"Contractors called. Apparently they had just been discussing asking you or any of us to help so she could open the restaurant faster. She was adamant that she didn't want our help, especially yours."

"What the fuck? Why?"

"Something about wanting to do it herself."

"Well, shit. I thought I was helping. Why wouldn't she want me to help?"

"How dare you!" Kayla stormed into his office.

Jake laughed into his ear. "Sounds like you're about to find out."

Evan ended the call and looked at Kayla, still trying to sort out what he had done wrong.

"You made decisions without even talking to me!" she yelled.

He stood and walked around her, closing his office door, before facing her again. "I was trying to be helpful and get the restaurant open again sooner."

"It's my restaurant. My decisions," she yelled, pointing to herself.

Evan took a deep breath, trying to keep calm because reminding her right now that they were both in charge of the restaurant's decisions wouldn't help. "It was supposed to a nice gesture."

"I don't want you spending your money on it. That's why I have insurance, Evan." She paced as she continued. "You just throw a bunch of money at it and it's all solved, but I can't do that for myself so now I owe you!"

Well, it didn't make sense, but at least he was getting to the bottom of the problem. "Kayla, the insurance will pay me back. It's not a loan to you. I would never have done anything to put you in debt to me or anyone else without your consent."

"You did!"

"I didn't. The insurance will pay it all back. It's just a matter of getting it moving faster."

"You don't get it!" she yelled.

He was sure the whole office could hear her raging through the door. "I don't," he agreed. "Explain it to me. I really was trying to make it better, not trying to upset you, at all."

Kayla sat on the edge of the leather sofa in his office, one knee bouncing as he waited for her to say something. He wanted so badly to go to her, but he held back, uncertain what to do.

"I needed to do this without you," she finally said.

Evan crouched next to her, putting a hand on her bouncing knee to still it. "Why?"

She blew out a breath but didn't pull away. "It's my problem, Evan."

"It's our problem, Kayla. I'm a partner in the business."

Kayla rolled her eyes. "A silent one."

"Okay. I don't understand your reservations here. Neither you nor the restaurant owes me any money from this."

"I need to be able to do this without you."

"Why?" he asked again.

"Because I need to be able to buy you out one day and own this. It's important, Evan. I told you that when I asked for help."

He remembered. It was one of the main reasons he'd agreed to help her. She had been so adamant that it was temporary, just to get the restaurant off the ground and have that backing.

"You still can." His gut clenched. Her wanting him out of the restaurant only showed where her thoughts were headed regarding him, and it wasn't good.

"I can't if the first time I come up to a real challenge you have to step in to help me," she told him.

He took a chance and sat next to her, putting his arm around her shoulders. "Kayla, going to your friends for advice, or help, or anything else doesn't mean you can't do it. It's a smart decision."

She shrugged. She didn't pull away, and he let that thought comfort him.

"Look at me." He waited for her to look up. "When things happen and one of us can help, we are always there for each other. Always. It doesn't mean we can't do it alone."

"I don't have anything to bring to help anyone," she mumbled.

"You're doing the date things with us. That was a whim, and you were ready to help. You stood up for Lauren the last time her mom and Cade's dad went crazy. You only need to be you," he told her.

"It's too much. Cade has security guards at my doors," she groaned. "And I don't even know who to thank for getting those doors boarded up. Then someone cleaned up most of the glass that was everywhere. I don't know who, so how do I pay any of that back?"

"You don't. No one expects it. I can tell you who helped with what if you really want to know, but they aren't expecting anything in return."

"That's how it works, Evan. People expect something in return."

"These people don't." He was learning a lot about Kayla. "I did not step in to help because I thought you couldn't do it. I did it because I'm your friend. It has nothing to do with profits or anything else. I just wanted to help."

"You feel bad about the other night," she accused him.

"What?" Shock wasn't strong enough for what he felt by that statement. He was completely blindsided. "Kayla, no. Do I wish things had turned out differently after that? Hell, yes. But I think you have more thinking to do to consider who you think I am if you think I'm trying to buy you into my bed."

He let go of her and stood, walking to the other side of his office, needing to put some distance between them.

"That's not what I meant," she tried.

"Then tell me what you meant because that hurt," he told her honestly. "Do I want to sleep with you again? Yes. But can you seriously tell me that you believe I wouldn't have done this a month ago? If you think that I'm the kind of person that is only helping you to sleep with you, then I don't know what to say."

Kayla bit her lip watching him before turning away. "I'm so screwed up."

"I think I've done well at respecting your space after having mind-blowing sex with you and then you telling me never again. I've done my best to still be your friend, and that's all I'm trying to do here."

Kayla nodded. "I'll call them back and get it started." She stood and walked to the door. "Thank you, Evan."

"Wait," he called after her. "Tell me, is that really what you think of me?" he asked.

"It's what I think of me," she answered.

"What does that mean? Talk to me, please."

"I have never had this tight of a group of friends, Evan. I still feel like I'm on the outside of everything, and I don't know why." She turned away from the door and faced him. "Hell, Catherine got us all matching pajamas just to drink in. I'm not sure how much more included I could be, but they're your friends, Evan."

"They'd be yours too if you'd let them."

"I've never had anyone who just did something nice to be nice. Never. Not big things anyway. I clearly am too screwed up for this."

"You aren't screwed up." He went to her, pulling her into his arms. "I promise no one wants anything from you. I'll sign everything over for the restaurant to you today if that's what it takes for you to believe me."

She shook her head but sank into his hug. "No."

"I will."

"I know. Please don't. I just need some time to come to terms with a few things, okay?"

"I told you, take all the time you need. That applies to everything. I'm sorry I did this without talking to you first."

"I'm sorry for all of this."

"Keep me posted on what's going on, and I promise, no more surprises," he told her before letting go.

She nodded and let herself out of his office.

Chapter Nineteen
Evan

"You sure you're playing the same game as us?" Cade asked.

Evan was on a losing streak. He hadn't won one hand. It was Friday night, and at this point, he wondered if he *was* playing the same game.

"He's too distracted," Luke pitched in. He raked in his winnings with a grin.

"Clearly, if you're beating him," Ryker threw out.

"Hey! I resent that," Luke argued.

"What is up with you? For real," Jake said seriously.

"The shit with the restaurant and Kayla. It's just a lot. It's been a long week." He picked up his beer and took a sip. "I think I'm done playing tonight."

"Probably smart," Cade agreed.

"What happened with Kayla?" Jake asked.

Evan took another sip and wished he was drinking something stronger. "Which thing?" he sighed.

"After she high-tailed it to your office to rip you a new one yesterday," Jake said. "Wait—is there something else?"

"We slept together," Evan admitted. Damn, he needed to talk to someone.

"Last night?" Jake asked?

"Monday. When I took her home."

"So wait, all this damage to the restaurant, and you insist on taking her home, and then you sleep with her finally?" Cade's stunned reaction summed it up perfectly.

"Yes. She invited me in. Then things kind of happened."

"Then what's the problem? I figured you'd be over the moon about it," Cade said.

"I was. Then she said we shouldn't do it again."

"Ah. And then you tried to win her over and that backfired." Jake nodded as he pieced things together.

"Pretty much."

"Wait, what did you do to piss her off?" Ryker asked.

"I fucking paid contractors to start work on the restaurant early."

"That pissed her off?" Ryker asked.

"Apparently she thinks she owes all of us something for helping out Monday, and I made it worse. I explained to her that the insurance would pay me back, but she's upset over it."

"She doesn't owe us shit," Cade said.

"That's what I told her. We're friends and she's included in that. That's just what friends do." Evan shrugged. "Apparently, she's never had anyone help her just to help. By the way, who cleaned up the glass?"

"The guards I hired did it. They said it was a hazard, so I told them to go for it," Cade said.

"That pissed her off too," Evan muttered.

"What the hell?" Cade stood. "Anyone need another?"

They all nodded and Cade headed to the kitchen.

"I can have Lauren talk to her?" Jake offered.

"I don't know if that would help. They're already talking anyway. Plus, if she finds out I told all of you what happened between us and then what she said, she'll probably be even more mad at me."

Jake nodded. "Okay."

Cade returned and handed everyone a beer.

"So, what happened in the bedroom? Was it bad?" Luke asked.

Evan rolled his eyes but answered anyway. "No. It was good. She got hers twice. Only had one condom so we slept after, and then in the morning, she was up early and gone from the bed before I woke up."

"Maybe it scared her. She admit to anything in bed?" Cade asked.

Evan thought it over. Nothing was out of the ordinary other than her liking it a little rough. "Not that I can think of."

"Did you?" Luke asked.

"No. I was a little dominant, but she seemed into it."

"Are you just accepting it?" Ryker asked, paying more attention than he normally did to anyone's relationship conversation.

"Of course not. I told her I'd give her space to think about it."

"So what happened yesterday then?" Jake pressed.

"She showed up panicked about the contractors. She yelled and then we talked through it mostly. When she left, she said she was going to call the contractors."

Everyone nodded, thinking. It was all he had to give them—that was everything that had happened, and he didn't know what to do with the information.

"Maybe try the blind date chick again?" Cade said.

"Yeah. See if another date gets your mind off things," Luke said.

"See? It was rational when Cade said it. When you say it, I wonder about the sanity of the idea," Ryker joked.

"I don't want to date anyone else," Evan admitted.

It wasn't a bad idea though. He'd had a connection with her in the app, but it felt like cheating on Kayla to text another woman.

"I say go for it. Even if Luke agrees. It might help you sort things out and make sure you want to keep waiting on Kayla to change her mind," Cade said.

Evan shrugged. "I don't know. I'll think about it." He looked over at Jake who had been quiet. "Nothing to add?"

"Nope," Jake said.

"It's your date pick then?" Evan asked.

Jake shrugged. "What you do is entirely up to you."

"Who is it?" Evan asked, knowing he wouldn't get an answer.

"Also nope."

"Worth a shot."

They settled back into the game and everyone went back to laughing and joking again. Evan had refused to play another hand but sat at the table with everyone.

He ignored them as he debated what Cade had said. Did he need to talk to his blind date? Would it help him sort things out? He didn't know.

What he did know was he couldn't fix anything just sitting there drinking. "I'm going to head home."

He slid away from the table and carried his empty bottles to the trash before heading out. Thankfully, he'd called a car here, planning to drink. He'd only had four but probably shouldn't be driving as distracted as he was right now.

The car met him out front and he slid in. He pulled out his phone and opened the app. He hadn't messaged K in a while, but she hadn't messaged him either. It had probably fizzled out before it even began anyway.

The ride home was short. He thanked the driver as they pulled up and told him he was done for the night. He needed to go inside and take a shower and try to figure out what to do.

That was the plan anyway. Cade's suggestion played in his head over and over as he debated what to do. He opened another beer and carried it with him to his room.

A quick shower had him feeling better, but his thoughts were still all over the place. He wanted to text Kayla, not some stranger. Which, if he were totally honest, said more than anything else.

He didn't need a test to see what was happening in his head; he knew what he wanted. But maybe he needed to talk to K to make sure. Or to at least confirm what he already thought he knew.

Then, what if she wrote back? It wasn't fair to her that he was more interested in someone else.

Torn again, he stretched out on his bed and stared at the app and the messages with K. They had gone so well in the beginning, but then their dates had been cancelled again and again. It wasn't because of either of them, but surely that was a sign?

Now he was thinking about signs! He was more screwed up than he thought. Texting to check on Kayla was an option, likely one that wouldn't be appreciated, though.

With a resigned sigh, he opened the app again and sent a message to K.

E: *Sorry I've been MIA. I feel like we keep getting pulled apart.*

There, he'd done it. Now he just needed to see if she wrote back.

Chapter Twenty
Kayla

Kayla stayed in for the night. Lauren had invited her over while the guys were at poker, but she wasn't good company right now.

She'd literally lost her shit on Evan in his office yesterday, and she was still reeling from the embarrassment of it all. She'd overreacted to everything, and he'd been so patient with her.

Worse, she didn't even mean to act like that. The emotions from the week had overwhelmed her, and she'd taken them all out on Evan. Him saving the day was the tipping point, and she'd lost it.

"I'm so stupid," she'd muttered to herself.

Avoiding Evan had been her goal since. She hadn't messaged him other than to tell him when the contractors were coming. Anything else was too much.

He hadn't reached out to her either, which was what she thought she wanted. Now she missed him.

So she'd stayed in and was doing her laundry having a real grand time on her Friday night. Sitting here, thinking about Evan, and refusing to do anything about those thoughts was only making herself more miserable.

The police had made no progress with her case. She called them that morning, and they basically told her to stop and they would call if they found something. It was valid, but she wanted to know why this happened and then to know that it wouldn't again.

She wasn't scared; she was pissed off. This was impacting her business and her livelihood. It also meant that customers could lose faith in her business, and this vandalism could give credence to the rumors that sometimes floated when people didn't like their dates.

Her phone chimed and she picked it up, intending to ignore whoever it was. It was the dating app with a message from Evan, or E to be more precise.

She opened it and took note of the apology. She shouldn't write him back, but if real her couldn't talk to him, maybe fake her could. She missed him.

Before she could change her mind, she wrote him back.

K: *I've been so busy with work. Sorry I haven't reached out more.*

She was curious where this was headed anyway. Honestly, she had forgotten all about the dates with everything else going on.

He didn't write back quickly so she went back to folding her laundry. She checked the phone entirely too many times while she did. Between each piece of folded laundry, she turned her phone over, looked for a message, and then set it back facedown on her bed.

It was unnecessary. Her phone clearly worked and made noise when he sent a message. Kayla fussed at herself as she stood and put her laundry away. She was being ridiculous.

She was in the middle of hanging up the pile of clothes at the end of her bed when her phone dinged again. Stopping immediately, she grabbed it to read his message.

E: *I've had a lot going on too.*

Yeah, dealing with her craziness. At least here, as K, she didn't have to talk about that. They could just chat.

She laughed at herself. What a difference from the first time they'd chatted in the app. She was so nervous then, but now she wanted it, needed to talk to him.

K: *It's nice to hear from you.*

K: *No big Friday night plans?*

E: *I was out at a friend's but I wasn't feeling it so I came home. You?*

K: *Even less exciting, doing laundry.*

E: *Oh, so you're a real partier, huh?*

She looked at the phone and regretted messaging him back. He was flirting. He slept with her four days ago and was flirting with someone else now?

K: *Yeah, real life of the party here.*

Kayla set the phone aside as she tried to figure out what she had done. This whole date thing was wrong. Messaging him back tonight had been a bad idea. The entire thing had been a bad idea.

She was learning more about her friend than she wanted. Like knowing that he would pursue two women at the same time. Yes, she had tried to back out of sleeping with him again, but he'd all but begged her to think about it, and now he was chasing another woman instead of waiting like he said he would.

Maybe it wasn't flirty. Was she overthinking it? Yes, maybe. Now she was overthinking her overthinking. Ugh. Apparently needing to punish herself, she picked up her phone and read his next message.

E: *I was playing poker and lost every single hand.*

K: *Oh no! I hope it wasn't a lot of money.*

E: *No, we keep it friendly, no big bets. It's all for fun.*

E: *Any plans for after your exciting laundry journey?*

K: *Need to eat some dinner, haven't decided what.*

E: *Cooking or ordering?*

K: *Cooking.*

E: *Can't help you then. I don't know what you have.*

K: *Something easy, for sure.*

E: *LOL.*

She went to the kitchen to see what she had to cook. It was late already, but she needed to eat.

Poking through her freezer, she found some popcorn shrimp and threw it in the oven. She loved those little things. Happy now that she was about to eat, she went back to the app.

Before she could send her message, her phone rang. Evan. She stared at it, almost letting it go to voicemail before giving in and answering.

"Hello?" she asked.

"Hey," he said.

The line went quiet and she waited for him to say something. He didn't.

"Is everything okay?" she asked.

"I know you probably don't want to hear from me. I just...miss you," Evan told her.

She slid into a chair. It was the same way she felt. "I've missed you, too."

"What are you doing?" he asked.

"Cooking some popcorn shrimp." Thankfully she hadn't sent the message and told him that as K.

"You're so weird," Evan laughed.

"Can't help it. They're good." He liked to tease her about liking them. "I thought you were at poker."

"Keeping tabs on me?" he teased.

"Lauren invited me over. I wasn't feeling it."

"I'm sorry," he told her.

"Don't be." It wasn't all his fault. It was hers.

The line went silent again and she had a thought. She wondered what he would do if K texted him right now. Putting him on speaker, she sent a quick message.

K: *What did you have for dinner?*

Just a test to see if he would message K while talking to her.

"Any information from the police?" Evan asked.

"Ugh. No. I called again, and they told me they'd call me if they had anything."

"Nothing from Jake either. They are looking to link it to Lauren's mom, but they can't find her. He's got a private investigator."

"Wonder what her plan is?"

"What do you mean?" Evan asked.

"It's just, I doubt that she's done. She didn't get anything out of it."

"Hmm." Evan was quiet. "I didn't think about it like that. It could have been just to shut the restaurant down."

"I thought that, too. But everything we know about her says she's after money."

"Yeah. I'll bring it up to Jake and see what he thinks."

"Thanks." The conversation lulled, and she waited for a chat to come through.

"Hey, Kayla?"

"Yeah?"

"Thanks for answering tonight."

She melted. "I don't want to not talk to you."

"Same. Can I ask you a question, though?"

"Shoot."

"Have you thought anymore about Monday?"

So much. "I haven't decided anything yet, but yes."

"I was worried you were going to hang up on me. I just needed to know that you were thinking about it."

"I am."

The oven beeped; her food was ready. She heard Evan laugh as she pulled the pan out of the oven.

"I'll let you go eat your kid food."

"Just because you can get it on a kid's menu doesn't mean that adults can't eat it," she defended playfully.

"Good night, Kayla."

"Good night, Evan."

The call ended, and she found she felt better than she had in a while. It was nice to talk to him again, even if the topics had been a little heavy at times.

Unable to resist the nagging thought that he was talking to her and K at the same time, she opened the messages as she ate. He hadn't written her back while they were talking or even after. That was a good sign, right?

On the other hand, he hadn't mentioned talking to K tonight either. She wasn't entitled to the information, and they had hardly discussed anything like being exclusive, but it felt wrong.

She went back to the main part of the app and requested setting up a date with him before sending one last message.

K: *I think we should meet.*

Now she just needed to wait for him to reply.

E: *You're right. I feel like what I want to say should be done in person.*

Pissed, she closed the app. Now she had to get through a whole week before their date that he had agreed to. He'd asked if she was thinking about Monday, and she'd been honest with him about it, and he went on and accepted another date instead. She wasn't pissed. She was hurt, and he was about to find out why.

Chapter Twenty-One
Evan

"I don't think you're playing the same game as us again," Cade teased.

It was Sunday afternoon, and he was at the basketball court with everyone. He was once again playing a game like crap.

"Very funny," Evan muttered and passed the ball.

"I'm just saying. Whatever you've got going on today certainly seems to be making things worse." Cade took a shot, making it. "I thought you'd have worn yourself out with Kayla on a run this morning."

"I tried. She's not answering." Evan had called her first thing this morning to see if she was going for a run, but his call had gone straight to voicemail. "With everything going on, I didn't want her to go alone."

"Well, she did. I saw her at the coffee place this morning, and she thanked me for my help with the security."

"What the fuck is going on?" Evan left the court and grabbed his phone from the bench, dialing her. Again, it went straight to voicemail.

"Did you do something last night to piss her off?" Ryker asked.

"No. We talked. It went well, I thought." Evan relayed their conversation.

"Out of curiosity, did you talk to your date in the app, too?" Jake asked.

"Yeah, a little. Nothing important. We discussed food."

"Anything else?" Jake asked.

"She messaged me while I was talking to Kayla, but I haven't written her back. Then she asked to set up a date, and I agreed after I got off the phone." Evan shrugged and took a seat. "I just figured I owed it to her after all the misses to meet her in person and break it off. With the restaurant closed, it'll have to be without the anonymity from Blind Date."

Cade whistled. "You don't owe a person you've never met anything."

"The conversations were good, but every time we got ready to have a date, something would happen with Kayla or the restaurant and I couldn't. It feels wrong to just text and break it off."

His friends grunted some reactions and then went back to their game, one man short. Evan sat on the bench and tried to piece together what had gone wrong.

He replayed the conversation over again in his mind. It didn't seem to matter how he did it, he couldn't come up with anything that sounded off in the conversation. They had finally talked and when they ended the call, nothing seemed weird.

Then a thought popped in his head—could she see that he had accepted a date? Probably, but why would she have looked? Unless she had some type of alert on.

He pushed the thought away. She wouldn't have an alert on for him. He doubted that was even a thing, and they had turned off email notifications for dates from the system because it was overloading her inbox as Blind Date became more popular, so she wouldn't have accidentally seen it in her email.

It wasn't a date for him. It was just a polite let-down of a bunch of almost dates and a few good conversations. He didn't know why, but he felt the need to meet up face to face to end things. Well, he would have preferred the restaurant and the darkness but that wouldn't happen for a while.

K seemed to be just as busy as he was with the chaos that had happened recently, so it wouldn't have worked between them anyway. They forgot to message each other and since each time he'd had to cancel their date, she'd also been busy, it was likely they'd never see each other.

Evan made a decision. If he didn't see her Friday as planned, then that was the end of it. He wouldn't try again to do things in person and just let her know that it wasn't going to work through the app. Jake could explain what was going on to her if he wanted since he was more than sure that his date was set up by him,

"Don't beat yourself up too much; she's got a lot going on, too." Jake sat next to him.

"I know. I just don't get it."

He was stuck somewhere between complete understanding and being angry at the mixed messages she was sending. It was getting really old.

"I'll ask Lauren if she knows what's up," Jake said.

He thought about it for a second and shook his head. "Don't worry about it. She will either tell me and give me a chance to fix it or she won't. I can't keep doing this."

Jake nodded his understanding. "I know how you feel. If it helps, I have a feeling this is one big miscommunication thing."

"Maybe, but I've been trying to figure out where, and I've come up blank."

"That's how it usually works and then when you find out, it's like it was right there obvious the whole time."

"Sure wish it would happen sooner rather than later."

"I understand that."

"How are things going with you and Lauren?" Evan asked, needing a subject change from his own drama.

"Really well. I think we will go the way of Owen and Jenna soon."

Evan smiled at his friends. "Congratulations!" He meant it; this was great news for them.

"I kind of want to sort out what's going on with her mother before we get there. I know that's weighing on her a lot."

"Oh, Kayla wondered what she might do next. Seemed to think she hadn't gotten any money out of doing this so there had to be something else in the works." And there he was, full circle, thoughts back to Kayla.

"We thought of that. The trouble is, we can't find her."

Evan nodded. "How is she hiding so well?"

"I think she's broke again already and places that let you stay for dirt cheap don't run credit cards or care what your name really is."

"Shit," Evan mumbled. "I don't know how we will figure that out then unless she pops up again."

"I really hope we are all wrong and it was just a tantrum. The last thing I want is more negativity on you guys and the restaurant because she's nuts."

"We don't blame either of you," Evan reassured him.

"I know, but it's still there, some guilt over it."

He could empathize with that. "Let me know if I can help with anything for the investigation. I know the police are working on it, too, but as far as we know, they haven't gotten anywhere."

"It's such bullshit. We have literal proof of who it is and still can't do a damn thing about it."

"Any luck figuring out who the men were?" Evan asked.

"None, their masks were covering them enough that no facial recognition would pick it up and they don't speak at all. They had a plan, executed it, and left." Jake toweled his face off and pulled his shirt back on. "I feel like we're missing something big here."

"Same. I have watched the footage a million times and I don't see anything there. I can't figure out where another clue would be that we're missing."

"I'm paying people to look into it, and they're coming up blank too."

Evan nodded.

"You guys talking about the restaurant?" Luke joined them.

"Yeah," Jake answered.

"Have you looked into anyone else that had bad dates? Like maybe someone was super mad and crossed paths with her?"

"We did. No one stood out." Evan sighed, nothing had stood out in anything.

Luke looked back to the court before lowering his voice and turning to them again. "Have we looked at Cade's dad again? I mean he was pissed, and I was shocked he let any of it go."

Evan scratched his beard as he thought about it. "I'd say probably not. I think he and Cade have come to an understanding since them. Plus, I never really understood the drama there to begin with."

"Separation of classes. It's one thing to fool around with a secretary; it's quite another to openly date one." Luke shrugged as if it all made sense.

"Hey." Jake punched his arm.

"I didn't say I agreed with him. Damn. We all love Lauren." Luke rubbed his arm.

"Yeah, but it wasn't his kid. He already openly doesn't like Jake, so it shouldn't have mattered."

"But, it was the same time that Cade started standing up to him. Plus, I was there almost every time that he did because I'd try to pull him out of meetings with his father," Jake said.

"Maybe. I still think it's old news, but it's worth looking into," Evan conceded.

"Should we tell Cade?" Luke asked.

"Let's see if we come up with anything to talk about first. I don't want him to know about it if we come up empty. There's no reason to add more stress to that relationship," Jake said. "I'll get my guys on it today."

"Thanks," Evan said. His phone rang and he reached for it, seeing Kayla's name. "It's her," he told Jake.

"See? It's going to be fine, just answer it."

Chapter Twenty-Two
Evan

The phone call was anything but good news. Now, an hour later, everyone was gathered at Evan's place, piecing information together.

The call from Kayla had been to tell him about a threat that she got. Everyone had rallied together and shown up. They were going to show their strength in numbers, and everyone had a skill to be used.

"Read it again," Ryker demanded.

"Send it to the projector, Kayla," Evan told her. "We can all spread out in the media room and she can put it up on the screen."

Kayla nodded and picked up her laptop, leading the way. He rarely used this room but in his defense, it came with the property and wasn't the reason he bought it. For now, it would serve as a good command station for everyone.

"Catherine's here, can someone go let her in?" Cade said looking at his phone.

"I'll go." Ryker headed off before anyone could say anything about it.

"Weird," Kayla muttered.

"Those two? A little weird," Evan agreed.

She was still being a little cold to him and didn't want to be alone with him, he'd noticed, but she was talking to him again, which was a step up from where they were just hours ago.

Cade stood in the middle of the room, reading the email on the screen, ignoring everyone around him as he did. Evan watched him, waiting to see what he came up with.

"This implies that they were able to get into your computer systems during the break-in. They didn't see you so I guess they didn't know you were there?" Cade asked.

"I don't think they did. They didn't touch the computers though. All the reservations and stuff are on tablets, and we lock those up at the end of night so they weren't even damaged," Kayla explained.

"They want money but there's no return of information. It doesn't seem that they thought this through at all." Cade looked back and forth between his phone and the screen.

"Well, we know my mother isn't one to think anything through. She cares about money and that's it. At least now we know what was up her sleeve," Lauren said.

"Something isn't right," Cade said again. "I don't know what it is, but something feels off."

"I think it's an empty threat. A play for money," Evan said.

"What if it's not, though?" Kayla asked. "If I don't pay and they do have the information they release, then I'm done. No one would ever come back."

Evan looked back over the email again.

Dear Kayla,

I was saddened to learn about the recent break-in at your restaurant. Information has come my way that may be valuable to you.

It seems that your business operates under certain conditions of anonymity. I am in receipt of a list of all the clients that patronize your facility and the dates that they have been on.

I am willing not to share this information for a price, of course. I expect that your restaurant has flourished and that, combined with your friends, you will be able to pay for this list to keep your business from being revealed.

I will be in touch again with the details of where to send the payment. In the meantime, you may work on gathering it all. I expect that the sum of $500,000 is not too high a price to pay to keep your secrets, as I am sure plenty of people would be upset if their names and dates were revealed.

There is no need to contact the police. They work too slowly to find out who I am, and I assure you that I will release the information to others who will pay for this type of gossip if you refuse to pay.

We will talk again soon,

Information Holder

It was from a random email address, nothing traceable at first glance.

"We need to call the police," someone said.

"It strictly says not to," Kayla argued.

"Technically, it says that it would be a waste of time," Evan said.

"While also saying that they would release the list to other people," Kayla argued.

"Well, you can't just pay them half a million dollars. They don't even say they're going to return this supposed information to you," Evan challenged her.

"If they have something and it gets out, it won't matter if I lost money to them or not because there will be no more restaurant," Kayla yelled back.

"Calm down, everyone. We aren't going to solve anything by arguing," Lauren said, playing mediator yet again.

"I will get this over to my investigators and see what they can find out," Jake told everyone.

"Fine," Kayla said. She folded her arms across her chest and took a seat. "So I guess now we just wait for more emails and see what happens?"

"It's the best of both worlds. We have investigators on it who aren't police," Evan said, trying to soothe her.

"I said fine," Kayla told him.

"Do it," Evan told Jake.

The only thing he could do right now was give her more space. Leaving her side, where he wanted to be, he went to Cade to see what he was doing.

"I'm looking through the surveillance to see if there was anything they could have done to get access to the information from down-stairs. It doesn't look like, but I want to be sure," Cade's gruff voice met him as he walked over.

"Thanks," Evan told him.

The rest of the day flew by in a flurry of activity. Catherine had drafted copies of several different e-mails to send to clients depending on the outcome of the situation. She also had a few press releases ready to go, heading it off or in response to bad news,

The overall assumption at this point was that there had been no way to access the information physically through the break-in. The wild card was determining if anyone had hacked into the systems.

Jake's investigators weren't skilled in that area, so there was no way to tell yet. They were working harder on locating Lauren's mom.

"I have a friend who can look into this for us," Catherine said. "He says he should be able to tell if anyone remotely accessed the data and if it was extracted. Does anyone have a problem with me telling him to go ahead?"

"Who?" Ryker glared at her.

Catherine looked at him, confused. "No one you know," she answered.

Ryker grunted and went back to looking at his computer.

"Go for it," Kayla said.

Catherine nodded and typed away on her phone. "He's on it. I told him it's an emergency so hopefully, we will have an answer quickly."

"Do you need anything from me?" Kayla asked.

"Nope, we just wait now."

Everyone went back to working on different angles. At some point, someone ordered pizza and everyone took a short break to eat.

It was later than Evan realized as people started to head out. He yawned and looked around for Kayla to check on her before she headed out.

Finding her took longer than expected. He thought for a minute that she had slipped out without taking to him. Instead, he found her in one of the comfortable lounge chairs in the media room asleep. She was curled up in a ball, her neck bent at an angle that would be sure to hurt in the morning.

"Going to wake her?" Cade asked.

"I think I'll leave her be," Evan said, still looking at her.

"Good luck. She's going to be in pain in the morning." Cade slapped him on the back. "I'm heading home. Let me know if you hear anything."

He walked Cade out as he debated what to do about the sleeping woman. On the one hand, if he left her, she was going to be in pain, but if he picked her up to carry her to a bed, she might get pissed.

Cade was the last one to leave, and he locked up after closing the door. Evan busied himself cleaning the kitchen and taking pizza boxes to the trash as he debated what to do. In the end, he decided there was no way he could just leave her there.

He went back to the media room and carefully scooped her into his arms. She shifted and curled into him, mumbling something as she did.

He carried her to his room and put her on the bed, pulling the covers up around her. He didn't dare touch her further and left her there sleeping. She hadn't woken at all so he could deal with whatever fall-out came tomorrow.

Without his bed, Evan went back to cleaning. The media room took a few minutes to put back to rights, and he turned the lights off with a silent prayer that they caught the person doing this soon.

Chapter Twenty-Three
Kayla

Kayla woke up in Evan's bed. It had taken her a minute to clear the fog from her brain and realize where she was. First, she had panicked, and then she had smelled him. It was calming and she knew where she was even before she climbed out of the bed.

Evan's scent was on one of the pillows on her bed, too. It was the only thing she hadn't washed from their night together, the scent of his soap and cologne soaking it through.

The last thing she remembered was being in the media room with everyone. She had been so tired from all the stress of dealing with this mess that she must have passed out. That meant Evan must have carried her to his bed.

She looked over, not sure what she expected, knowing he wasn't in the room. The bed was still made on the other side, which meant he'd given up his bed for her and slept somewhere else.

Her phone was charging on the side table, something she was incredibly grateful for. She unplugged it and checked to see if the blackmailer had emailed her again yet. Nothing.

She stretched and got up. She needed to apologize to Evan for taking his bed and to thank him at the same time. He could have left her in the recliner, but he hadn't for whatever reason. It was sweet and if she didn't already know better about him, she'd be flattered.

Evan was in his office down the hall, his voice traveling to her as she opened the bedroom door. She considered for a minute just leaving a note and slipping out but then convinced herself she was better than that.

Kayla walked to the open office door and knocked on the doorframe quietly to get his attention. He smiled and waved her in.

"Hey, she's awake, let me call you back after I talk to her," Evan said. He ended the call and sat the phone down on his desk. "Good morning."

"Thanks for putting me in a bed last night," she told him.

"Your neck was going to hurt if I didn't. It was at the worst angle."

"I was wondering why you moved me. Thank you again. Sorry I fell asleep on everyone."

"You were exhausted. I hope you slept okay?"

"Well enough." She had slept hard and it was overdue. She needed it.

"I'm glad to hear it." He stood and picked up his phone, walking over to her. "Jake thinks he might have a lead on where she's staying."

Kayla smiled. "I hope so. It would be so nice to wrap all of this up and move on."

"Agreed."

"I think I want to go through the footage again today and see if anything feels off. I know Ryker did yesterday, but I know the restaurant better than anyone, and I just feel like I need to find something."

Evan nodded. "Hook it up in the media room and watch it on the big screen. We've all watched it more than once on computer screens, so it might help to change the perspective."

She nodded. Her intention wasn't to stay here and do it but he had a point. "I'll get out of your way and do that, then."

"Kayla, what's happened?" he asked.

She sighed. "Not now, Evan." He'd find out on Friday when his date was her.

"Fine. Let's go," he said.

"You go back to work. I can look at it alone."

"This is all I have worked on this morning. Come on, we can eat something and then both take a look."

She trudged along after him. He'd taken her reasons to leave and boxed them up with solutions, and she wanted to scream. She'd eat and then do one run through of the footage and then she'd leave.

Evan got to work in the kitchen, apparently preparing to make a full breakfast. He got out eggs and pans, and she looked anywhere but at him.

"I was thinking we could also review access to the server. I know we kind of did last night, but what if they got your login info somehow? We should check where the different logins were from," Evan told her as he cooked.

She thought it over and agreed. "Probably a good idea. We were looking for anyone else to access it last night."

He nodded his acknowledgment and kept cooking. A few minutes later, two pieces of toast, eggs, and bacon were placed in front of her, along with a cup of coffee. She thanked him and ate quickly.

She felt surprisingly better after that. Now she just needed a shower and she'd probably even feel more awake. That would have to wait till she got home though.

"Which one do you want to start with?" he asked.

"The cameras, please. Do it all four at once, please? Since we have it on the big screen, I'd like to watch them all at the same time."

She settled into a chair and pulled her feet up next to her as Evan put it up on the screen. He took another seat and watched with her.

It was hard to see the split version on her computer monitor. From here, they could clearly see what everyone was doing.

"Pause it!" she shouted, sitting up.

"Okay." Evan jumped up and went back to the computer they were casting the images from.

"Go back a few frames," she told him, watching carefully at Lauren's mother. "There!"

Kayla jumped up and went to the screen.

"What?" Evan asked.

"Look at her. Go back a few more and then hit play, but watch her." She pointed at the screen.

Evan did. "Damn."

"She's talking to someone. It's so subtle." Lauren pointed at it again.

"If we weren't watching it this big, we never would have seen that."

"I thought she was mumbling to herself, but watch her eyes. Someone is standing out of the camera range."

"They're letting her take the fall for this and staying out of the way. Dammit!"

Evan grabbed his phone and called someone, telling them what they had found. She stared at the screen, watching for any movement as it continued to play in front of her. Hopefully, they would see something, a reflection in the car, something to tell them who they were dealing with.

"Jake's on it," Evan told her as he ended the call.

"Keep playing it. Take it just to this one shot."

He removed the split screen and Kayla backed away from the screen so she could see it better. They spent another half an hour reviewing the clip from before they arrived until well after they were gone. Whoever she spoke to knew where the cameras were.

"That has to be who emailed me," Kayla said. "It was too professional sounding to be Lauren's mother I think."

"That's what Cade was saying last night. It seemed like it wasn't from her—it was nowhere near demanding enough."

"Not needy."

"Exactly," Evan agreed and then cut off the video. "I'll pull up the access records now and see if we have anything on there we can sort out."

She waited as he did. It was mostly timestamps and IP addresses, not something she was going to be much help with.

"Okay, let me do something," Evan said thoughtfully from the back of the room.

He sorted the list and then plugged in some numbers, hiding some results.

"What did you do?" she asked.

"That is the IP address of the restaurant. I'd say it was safe to assume the other one that is in here often is your house, so I'll exclude that one too."

"There are only a few others but they're old. They could be my work or my house from when we were setting everything up. Nothing unknown that was recent."

"But then if they used the restaurant to get to it, it would have been in the ones we excluded."

"Possibly, not the tech guy in this scenario." He punched a few more numbers in. "That eliminates my house, but again, they're really old logins."

"So this was a bust for looking up."

Evan nodded. "It was worth a shot."

She agreed. "Have you heard anything from Catherine or her guy?" Kayla asked.

"Not yet."

"I haven't heard from the blackmailer again. What if they really have something? I can't just let them ruin this."

"We will get to the bottom of it. Everyone is working on it that we know. Something will happen to confirm they never had access to the system."

"What if they did?"

"Then we will cross that bridge when we get to it. I really don't think they were able to get in, though."

"I don't either, but I'm not willing to risk everything on thoughts, Evan."

"We aren't paying them right now," Evan told her.

"I can't pay them anyway. We need to come up with something that we can do if they got in."

"Look, this system is secure. We know this. It was the main reason we chose it."

Kayla shrugged. It didn't matter what he said. She needed to make a plan for something bad to happen. She felt it coming and couldn't ignore it.

She checked her phone once more to see if she had heard from the blackmailer again. "Evan, they wrote me again." Her hands shook as she tried to click on the email.

Evan came up behind her and rubbed her arms, lending her some of his strength as he looked over her shoulder.

Kayla,

I hope you've had enough time to get the money. My banking details are enclosed in the attachment. If not paid, I will release the details to the gossips.

Information Holder

"I'll call everyone."

Chapter Twenty-Four
Kayla

Kayla didn't stay at Evan's much longer after they'd gotten the email. She also hadn't been back to the restaurant. The contractors had started work, and she checked their progress using the cameras for now, not wanting to get in the way.

She officially had doors again and all the glass had been replaced. They had also started tearing things out of the dining room that were too damaged to repair. It broke her heart to watch on the camera, and there was no way she could go see it in person right now.

A bottle of wine was her company for tonight as she made an elaborate dinner from scratch. It was taking her mind off things and giving her hands something to do.

Evan had called earlier to say that there was still no update from anyone. Her blackmailer hadn't given her a time to send the money, and Catherine's friend was trying to get information on the account itself.

So far, all was quiet. The fact that nothing was happening made her more nervous than if they were getting any information. It was as if they were in the calm before the storm, waiting on the next bad thing to happen.

She sipped her wine as she waited for her water to come to a boil for the pasta she was making. Everything else was done, and she was ready to eat, tempted to turn her phone off for a few minutes while she did.

Everyone had convinced her to wait it out. That the threat was nothing and they had no information to hand out. Catherine's guy had an emergency so they hadn't been able to confirm anything.

Her stomach was in knots just wondering at the choice she had made to ignore the emails. It wasn't like she could have paid them anyway. The restaurant was successful, but it didn't have half a million dollars sitting around.

Sipping her wine, she waited for what was going to happen next. She hated it.

Her water boiled, and she dropped the pasta in just as her phone started ringing.

"Hi Catherine," she said as she answered.

"Hey. How are you?" she asked.

"I don't know. It's just a lot. I owe you an apology for the other day, by the way. Sorry for being such a bitch."

Catherine laughed. "You already apologized but there's no need. You're under a lot of stress right now so I get it."

"Any chance you've heard from your guy?" Kayla asked.

"He's back in town, so I hope to have an update soon. I'm sorry it's taking so long."

"Can't complain about someone doing us a favor." It wasn't like she knew anyone else to ask anyway.

"Any word from your blackmailer since last night?"

"Nothing yet. I'm really worried. I know we don't think they have information, but what if they do?" Kayla stirred the pasta as she thought about it.

"It won't come to that," Catherine assured her.

"Everyone keeps saying that, but I can't help but feel like something's wrong." It was there, nagging at her, that this wasn't over.

"It's just the stress of the situation. And if something happens, we already have a PR plan to attack it," Catherine reminded her.

"Yeah, but it will break the trust that Blind Date has with the clients. I don't know that it could recover from that."

"It will. If it happens, it will. I know it's easier said than done, but don't stress it. That part is my job, and I'm damn good at it."

"No, please, don't be humble," Kayla teased her friend. "Hang on a second, I need to strain the pasta."

She set the phone down on the counter and picked up the pot, pouring it into the colander in the sink. Returning the pasta to the pot, she took it back to the stove and poured the sauce she made onto it.

Grabbing her phone, she noticed several alerts had shown up while she was talking. Emails, tons of them.

"Catherine?" She put the phone back to her ear.

"What's wrong? Are you hurt?" Catherine rushed out.

"I have a million emails. I'm going to get my laptop now."

"Shit. I'm getting dressed. Do you have wine? Or something stronger?"

"I don't know if it's bad yet," Kayla tried to convince herself.

"Now you want to be positive?" Catherine asked.

"Shut up." She put the phone on speaker and logged into her computer. Scrolling she saw clients names that she recognized and none of them were good subject lines. "It's not good."

"I see. It doesn't look like anything's been released from my quick search. Just a claim that they could. Anything from your blackmailer?"

"Not that I can see yet. There are so many emails, Catherine." She hated the quiver that had slipped into her voice. Tears were threatening.

"Call Evan. I'm on my way." Catherine ended the call.

Kayla gave herself a minute to pout before she did. She didn't want to call him, or anyone for that matter. It wasn't personal, she was just exhausted from being the one in trouble and calling everyone.

Friends were great, but they could only stand so much of her shit. Hell, she was getting tired of it. She debated texting him, but she wasn't that much of a coward. Opening his contact, she clicked call.

"What's wrong?" Evan answered.

She laughed, he wasn't wrong but it just showed how bad everything had gotten for him to answer like that. "I was right."

"Right about what?" Evan asked.

"It's public. Well, the threat is public. I have so many emails that I'm scared to even open one. They just keep coming."

"What the fuck?" Evan yelled on the other end of the phone.

"Catherine is on her way, but since it will effect you too, I wanted to let you know."

"I'm on my way, too. Do we need anyone else?"

"You don't have to come," she pushed.

"Don't do this right now, please? I'm coming. It's our business, and I'm going to be there. If you don't want me at your place, then everyone can come to mine, or the restaurant, or, hell, go neutral and use Catherine's office, but you're not blocking me out of this."

She listened and swallowed. He had a point, and she was being petty. "Here. I've had wine so I don't want to go anywhere if I don't have to."

"Then I'm on my way over," Evan said.

The call ended and she struggled to do anything. It was like she was frozen as the full shock sunk in while she was waiting on people to come and tell her what to do. Catherine had a plan, she'd even worked on it with her, but she couldn't remember what to do.

Dinner was completely forgotten. She sunk further into the sofa, wishing she could sink all the way in and stay there. It was awful. She didn't look at the emails anymore.

Tilting her head back, she stared at the ceiling and willed it to fall. It would be an improvement to everything else right now. This was becoming too much.

Eventually, Catherine knocked her tell-tale knock, letting Kayla know who it was. She opened the door for her to find Evan in the hall as well.

"Come on in." Kayla held the door wide for them.

Evan stepped in, took a look at Kayla, and hesitated. "It's going to be okay," he said. He raised his hand like he was going to reach out to her but then dropped it back to his side and went the rest of the way inside.

Kayla closed the door and turned to them. "I haven't opened any emails." She was scared to open them and see what everyone was saying.

"That's okay. We have a plan, remember?" Catherine pulled her laptop out and sat at the table.

"Wanna fill me in on that?" Evan asked.

"It's nothing special. Kayla had insisted that we come up with how to handle it if things went wrong. I need to adjust since no information was released, but I think we can make that work even better."

"Okay," Evan said.

"Just update my statement to say I was there. It's the truth and adds to the no-information bit," Kayla joined them.

"You'll need to go through your emails; we can set up an automatic reply. Get your employees notified first, and then reply to the ones that came in. Also, check for any from the blackmailer. They didn't give you a deadline, so it's weird that they went with this show of force so quickly," Catherine told her.

"Evan, can you go through the emails? I can't look at them," she asked. If he was here, then he could do that for her.

"On it," Evan said. He reached for the laptop. "Shit, I didn't bring mine, we can't both work on the same one."

"I've got my tablet," Kayla said. She slid her computer in front of him and then stood to go to her room for the tablet.

"The blackmailer sent a new one!" Evan yelled.

Chapter Twenty-Five
Kayla

"What does it say?" Kayla ran back into the room. Looking over Evan's shoulder, she read the message.

Kayla,

I had believed you to be smarter than this. Imagine my disappointment when no money came through to the account. Disappointment goes both ways, though.

I have not released any of the details to the gossips yet, but I will. You have until Friday to wire the money through. Make no doubt that I will release all the information if you do not pay this time. I trust you to make the right decision this time.

Awaiting my money,

Information Holder

"Information holder?" Evan shook his head. "Should we write them back?"

"No," Catherine told him. "There are bigger things to worry about right now. I'm adjusting the plan, but I have another idea I want to work on. I'll let you both know what it is when I work it all the way out."

"Can you check in with your hacker guy?" Kayla asked.

"I emailed him on the way over. As soon as he has something, he will let us know."

Gathering gave Evan a blurb to send to all the emails that had come in and set it as the auto-reply. While he worked on that, Kayla emailed all the employees to let them know that they were working on this and would be in touch soon with more details.

Kayla then reached out to her assistant to get her in the loop of what exactly was going on. Any questions that came her way were to be directed to Catherine instead. It didn't take long and she had completed everything.

"Did you ever eat?" Catherine said, looking up at Kayla.

"No." She should at least put it away. There was always tomorrow.

Standing, Kayla arched her back and stretched.

"Go ahead and eat," Evan encouraged.

"I'm just going to put it away. Not hungry anymore."

"You should eat something," he urged.

The thing was, she wanted to stay mad at him but couldn't. She should be annoyed that he was kind of telling her what to do, but she knew deep down that it was out of concern.

"I'll have a banana," she relented. It was too late for a big meal now, and she was too stressed for it.

He nodded and went back to the computer. Too quickly, she put dinner away and loaded her dishwasher. Joining them at the table again, she sat next to Evan and checked on the emails.

"They're bad, aren't they?" she asked.

"They aren't good," Evan told her.

The one he had open was someone threatening to sue her, so not good was an understatement to say the least.

Catherine's phone rang. "Oh, it's him!" She snatched it up and answered.

Kayla and Evan watched as she talked to him. She asked lots of questions and then finally asked if he could email her the details.

She grinned as she ended the call. "There is no reason to think that anyone accessed the system. He added that you should work less, Kayla. Nothing out of the ordinary had been done and there are no instances of information being downloaded by anyone. That includes the backup servers."

Kayla swayed and Evan spun sideways, pulling her into his lap. "It's okay, baby. That's really good news," he soothed.

She barely registered Catherine excusing herself as the stress and worry melted away. Nothing was done by any means, but at least she could confirm there was no breach. All the security on her end was still in place and no information was out there.

Evan continued to hold her, his hand making small circles on her back as he whispered soothing words to her. She relaxed into him for the moment, telling herself it wouldn't be for long. She just needed the support right now.

Kayla took a deep breath and stood. "Sorry," she mumbled as she slid into the other chair.

"You looked like you were about to fall," Evan told her.

"I was. It means a lot to know that the information hasn't gotten out."

"It does. We can keep looking into who the blackmailer is, but they can only threaten. There's nothing they can actually do. It's good news."

Catherine poked her head around the corner. "You guys, decent?" she teased.

They both gave her an awkward laugh.

"Okay. Onto the rest of the information." Catherine took her seat again. "He's still trying to see who the email belongs to, but he is also looking into the account information."

"Thank you," Kayla told her. "Really. Tell mysterious man the same thing, please."

"Mysterious man?" Catherine laughed. "He'll like that."

"Out of curiosity, have I met him?" Evan asked.

Catherine's eyes got wide and she nodded.

"Are you teasing Ryker on purpose?" he asked.

"No! I swear. I just didn't want to put his name out there."

"Hi. Lost over here," Kayla said.

"She's using Ryker's security firm to do this. I'd guarantee that her mystery man is his IT guy," Evan explained.

Kayla snorted. Leave it to Catherine to find a way to get under Ryker's skin.

"I didn't want to put his name out there and then Ryker yell at him for doing this favor for me," Catherine said, trying defending herself.

"As though Ryker would be mad at him for helping us?" Evan rolled his eyes.

"He'd be mad I had Thomas's number," Catherine said quietly.

"That part I believe. What are you going to do when he finds out?" Evan asked.

"Nothing. You aren't going to tell him so he has no reason to know." She glared at him.

"Woah." Evan held his palms up in mock surrender. "I never said I was going to tell him."

Kayla laughed as they went back and forth over it. It was nice to finally feel a bit relaxed.

"What about you two? Don't act like I didn't just see her on your lap." Catherine arched an eyebrow at him.

"She damn near fell. Next time you have big news, maybe wait till everyone is sitting down," he fussed at her.

"Mm-hmm." Catherine yawned and looked down at her watch. "Oh wow, I didn't realize it was past midnight already. I'm going to head home and tomorrow, or later today, we can meet at my office and discuss the next steps."

Kayla looked at her clock. She didn't realize how late it had gotten either. "You are welcome to crash in the spare room," she offered.

"No thanks. I'm going to head home, and then I'll set up a time to meet." Catherine closed her computer and stood. "Evan, check in with Jake when it's an appropriate time and see if his investigation has gotten anywhere. If not, I may ask Ryker for support there."

"Agreed. I can ask Ryker though. I don't want you to put yourself in a weird place," Evan told her.

"Thanks." Catherine put her laptop into the big bag she'd carried over tonight and headed for the door. "You'll be back up and running in no time, Kayla."

She genuinely hoped so. This idea had taken so long to launch and get to a successful point. All she wanted was to be able to run her business and own it outright.

"Are you going to be okay?" Evan asked.

"I'm good. I might even get some sleep tonight."

"I can stay if you want," Evan offered. "I mean on the sofa or your spare room," he rushed out.

She wanted him to leave, right? Maybe. She knew she'd sleep a heck of a lot better with him here—hell, even better with him in her bed. No. That wasn't going to happen.

"Either way is fine. You don't have to stay."

"I'd like to if you're okay with it." Evan looked at her but she looked anywhere else, staring out the window at the moment.

"Okay. I'm going to lock up then and head to bed. You know where everything is."

With that, she escaped to her room and closed the door. She should have told him to leave, she fussed at herself. There was no point in letting him stay other than to break her own foolish heart yet again.

The thing was, it really would help her sleep to have someone she trusted out there. She knew he would never let harm come to her as long as he could stop it. It was her heart she couldn't trust him with.

Kayla crawled into bed, her phone on silent, and stared at the ceiling. Sleep overtook her quickly, and she slept harder than she had in a week. Thoughts of Evan swirled in and out of her dreams, but no nightmares haunted her.

Chapter Twenty-Six
Evan

Evan had slept on Kayla's sofa last night, and oddly enough, he felt pretty rested this morning. He had been surprised that she had let him stay without arguing. He was fully prepared for her to say no and he was just going to leave.

Instead, she'd agreed and then ran away. She must have been more affected by the break-in than she had let on to anyone. It was the only reason he could think of that she would so readily agree to letting him stay, even if she made it sound like a casual indifference.

He stretched and ran a hand over his face. She hadn't made any noise yet, so he assumed she was still sleeping. He took his time in her guest bathroom, splashing water on his face and brushing his teeth. He was grateful she had stocked it to have extra things in case someone stayed over.

Finished, and more awake, he headed to the kitchen. The first order of business was coffee. He got it started and then rummaged through her fridge for breakfast ingredients, grinning to himself as he found everything he needed to make some French toast.

It was her favorite and super easy to make. He set about getting it together as quickly and quietly as he could. It was late morning now, and he knew that despite the late hour they went to bed, she would likely be up soon just like him. They were both naturally pretty early risers.

He called Jake while he cooked to ask for an update. His plan had been to wait for her to wake up before he did, but he had worried she might forget he had stayed over and hear him moving around and panic. Nothing to base that on, but he wanted her to know he was still here.

"Hey," Jake answered.

"Hey. Any luck?" Evan jumped right into it.

"Maybe, actually. There are two leads that they are tracking down today, and if either one proves to be her, we can have her arrested."

Evan smiled. Things were finally beginning to take a turn. "Fingers crossed."

"Right? I hope it's her so we can move on from this mess."

"Agreed."

"Did you see what the blackmailer did?" Evan asked.

"No?"

Evan explained what happened last night and then all the work the three of them had put in.

"Shit. You guys should have called. We would have helped, too."

"I know. Kayla has just really been through the wringer lately, though."

"She really has. How's she taking the news?"

"Damn near collapsed when we got word none of the data had actually been breached. I stayed on her couch last night, and we are meeting with Catherine at her office at some point today."

"Well, I'll let you know if either of these leads pans out today. The police will too if it works out and they arrest her."

"I hope so. I'll talk to you later."

"Later, man."

Evan ended the call right as he pulled the last piece of French toast off the pan. He hoped today continued in the good way it was trending. They needed this good news.

"Morning." Kayla walked into the kitchen.

"Good morning. I made French toast." Evan pointed to the two plates on the island. "Literally just finished. Coffee too."

She had clearly not been out of bed long, still looking a little confused. He wanted to pull her to him, hold her, carry her back to bed. None of which he could do until she made up her mind about him. He just wished it weren't taking so long.

"Thanks," she mumbled and walked past him to the bar.

"I'll get you some coffee." He poured her a cup and took the seat next to her on the bar with his own. "I called Jake this morning. He said they have two leads they are running down this morning. With any luck, one of them is her and they will have her arrested."

"I hope so," Kayla said between bites. "Thanks for this. It's really good."

"You're welcome."

His phone rang and he pulled it out of his pocket. Catherine was calling.

"Hello. You're on speaker with me and Kayla," he answered.

"I've tried Kayla a few times this morning, but she didn't answer. I was going to ask you to check on her, but I guess she's fine."

"Sorry. I put my phone on do not disturb when I went to bed last night," Kayla said.

"All good. Can you guys be at my office in an hour and a half?"

"Is everything okay?" Evan asked.

"No new developments," Catherine said.

"Jake's investigators have two leads they are running down. With any luck at all, they will track her down today," Evan said.

"God, I hope so," Catherine said. "I'll see you two shortly."

Evan ended the call and went back to his breakfast. "I'll clean this up before I head out. Unless you want to carpool?"

Kayla shook her head. "You go, I will clean it up since you cooked and then get ready."

He nodded and took his plate to the sink. "Are we ever going to talk?" Evan asked her.

"After this is done, Evan. I can't do this right now," she told him.

"Holding you to it," he said.

He got his shoes on and left her alone in her apartment. She hadn't said no, so he'd take that as optimistic and let it go. She did have a lot going on, that much was true, and he didn't want to add to it, but it felt like they were dancing around each other.

It didn't take long to get home and shower. He checked in on work while he passed the time before going to Catherine's. After answering a few emails, he called Catherine.

"Hey," she answered.

"Should I tell everyone to come? It just occurred to me to ask."

"Probably not. I told Cade because he's upstairs, but I didn't think to tell anyone else. What's Kayla say?" she asked.

"I didn't ask her yet. Thought I would check with you before asking her. She's still at home, I had to come home and change."

"Cade might come down, but I think that's probably all we need for now. We can make sure everyone else knows after."

"Okay. Just double-checking."

"Evan?" Catherine asked as he was about to end the call. "Go easy on my friend. I won't pretend to know everything between you two, but I can tell something is up."

He let out a self-deprecating laugh. "I think you have it backward there. I want to be with her, Catherine. It's Kayla that can't make up her mind. I know she's got a lot going on and I don't know how much you know, so I won't say more, but the ball is in her court."

"It seems a lot like the ball is in her court for everything," Catherine mused.

"I'm trying. I've been stuck between enemy and friend and something more for a while now. I know what I want, but she has to decide what she wants."

"Fair enough," she conceded. "I'll see you shortly."

Did everyone think he was messing with her feelings? His friends knew from the other day some of what was going on, but who else? Damn.

He grabbed his jacket and headed out. There was no point sitting at home worrying about everything. If he was early, then he'd go see Cade.

Traffic had picked up with the lunch hour, and it took him longer to get to her office than he expected. By the time he showed up, he only had about five minutes to spare. Kayla was already there.

"Perfect. Cade is stuck in a meeting, but he's nosy so we will probably see him before all is said and done." Catherine talked as they followed her to a conference room. "I really think this is the best way to handle everything, but if either of you has a problem with it, we can make changes, like always."

She unlocked her laptop which was being projected onto a screen at the other end of the room. After a few clicks, she had pulled up a presentation.

Evan was impressed as he looked over the sheets she passed to them. She had put this together in less than a day and had it board-room ready. He made a mental note to send her a gift card to some spa place—she needed a break.

"Okay. First thing is our press release. Here is the one that we had come up with before at the top. It still applies, but I think the new one on the bottom is more effective. Let's hit the blackmailer where it hurts and get the information out to everyone. I want to release the emails you've gotten and then the report from Thomas that nothing was hacked or downloaded. Proof that your security systems are up to par and working."

"Thomas?" Cade laughed from the doorway. "You have Ryker on a mission to figure out who your hacker man is, and it's his hacker man?"

Cade wiped his tears of laughter as he came in and took a seat.

"Don't tell him," Catherine pleaded.

"Oh, no worries there. I'm interested to see how long he keeps it up now that I know the answer." He continued to chuckle as she slid him a stack of papers. "We are just getting started, and I am going to assume you heard my pitch?"

"Yes. Proceed."

Catherine stuck her tongue out at her brother. "Anyway. I also want to release the police report and your statement, proving that you were there and there was no way anyone could have accessed anything. This will show that it's all made up."

Kayla flipped through the papers. "I don't know."

"What are you thinking?" Catherine asked.

"I know we have something, which I'll be the first to admit that I don't understand, that says no one accessed the data, but there's still the risk of the information being out there," she said.

"If it would make you feel better, I can set up a meeting with Thomas or a video chat and he can explain everything to you. I don't know all of it either, but I do trust him completely, as does Ryker, so I believe him if he says he's sure no one accessed the data." Catherine took a breath. "As your friend and PR rep, I do need to stress that the faster we move, the better."

"What can we do to restore trust, though?" Evan asked.

"Next page," she instructed. "Kayla, you let me know what you want to do about the statement later. I want to run the ads again of Jake and Lauren. Evan, I want you to come out with a statement that you've been using it and have complete trust in the system, along with anyone else we can recruit. The more prominent the person, the better."

"I know a few people who will help," Evan said.

"Great. Confirm they will and give me their information. Then the next page is full of potential ads I think you should run. I am not an expert in marketing, so you would need someone else to set these up and quickly, but I recommend running ads everywhere about how Kayla protected the information. Work with your tech companies that provide the security, hosting, and systems to partner in ads to show that you have done everything and how secure their systems are."

"How long did you work on this?" Cade asked.

"Came up with it last night," Catherine told him proudly.

"It's good," Cade said. "Not to inflate your ego, but I can't find any holes in the plan. Marketing could take a bit to get going and some customers may not come back, but it looks like the impact could be minimal here."

"Awe, such high praise," Catherine said, sarcasm dripping from her.

"Evan?" Catherine asked.

"I'm all in," he confirmed. It was a solid plan.

"Kayla?" she asked.

She nodded. "Fine. Do it."

Catherine did her giddy clap. "If you go to the next page, you'll see what I want to send to the customers is basically a copy of the press release. I'd like to send it out to them first just so they feel more in the know."

They went over the small logistics involved and before he left, there was a fully fledged plan in Catherine and Kayla's hands ready to launch.

Chapter Twenty-Seven
Evan

Thursday was spent launching all Catherine's plans. Evan didn't have much that was needed from him, so he finally went back to work for most of the day.

They consulted a marketing firm to do the ads that Catherine requested, but Evan had left that up to them to sort out. He had full trust in them to make the right decisions, and now that the drama was dying down, he was backing off more as Kayla wanted.

It killed him. Not the silent partner bit—he was a silent partner in more businesses than he could count off the top of his head. It was the fact that he had no reason to even talk to her now if he left himself out of the business.

He wanted to talk to her. He also had his break-up date tonight with K. She seemed like a good person, but he hadn't heard from her since she requested the date, driving home the point even more that they weren't a good fit. He was too interested in Kayla to care, but he didn't want a scene from K either.

Jake's investigators had managed to follow up on one lead, which was a bust. It looked like they might have better luck on the other one, but they were still waiting to confirm. He didn't ask any other questions about it.

At this point, as much as he wanted her caught, the urgency had died down since they confirmed no data was stolen. He wouldn't say it could take forever, but he was less pressed about it.

He searched the internet periodically to see how things were going. So far it seemed that most of the outlets had picked up the narrative that they were putting out there and the blackmailer was being shamed in comments.

Tomorrow he was going to get away for a little while if everything was still looking up. He didn't think Kayla would be ready to talk to him yet, so leaving and removing himself from everything that reminded him of her was his next best option.

Just a nice long weekend somewhere far away. He might ask Jake where he had taken Lauren and go there. A beach sounded nice. A nice cold beer and his feet in the sand would certainly take his mind off things.

His reminder about the date went off, and he checked his emails one more time, replying to a few. He should be proud that his office had run so smoothly without him in the last few weeks while he'd been so distracted, but it was one more thing that seemed not to need him.

When he got back, he'd look for a new investment. Something to immerse himself in and build up from scratch. He loved doing it, and it was a time-consuming process.

He shrugged into this jacket and walked over to the mirror, adjusting his yellow tie. They'd both agreed to wear yellow in the date settings so they could recognize each other. Hopefully, nothing was going on that had a bunch of other people wearing it, too.

They did have the app to talk to each other if they couldn't find each other. It was a real blind date this time, and he found it weird to think he might see her in person. Not because he was nervous, but just because she'd been one date and a handful of conversations. Up until tonight, she bordered on fictional to him.

He wasn't driving tonight, instead opting for a car just in case things went south, as it would make it easier to leave. With the other two dates going as they did, he couldn't put anything past anyone anymore.

Evan made a mental note to tell everyone that he was done with the blind dates for now. It had been an experience, to say the least, and as much as he wanted to settle down with one woman, it wasn't in the cards for him right now unless Kayla wanted the same thing from him.

He didn't care who was left to set him up; he wasn't ready. His friends would understand and if nothing else, he could tell Kayla via text that he was done.

She was on his mind as he made his way down to the waiting car. He gave in and sent her a text before he made it to his date.

Evan: *How's it going? Any news from the blackmailer?*

Kayla: *Good and nope.*

These were the kinds of responses he got from her now, and he worried it might be all he ever got again. If she would just talk to him, he might be able to fix whatever it was he'd done, but with the way things were, he didn't even know where to start.

"We're here," his driver said.

"Thank you. I don't know how long I'll be," he reminded him.

"That's okay. I will find a place to park. Just let me know when you're ready."

Evan nodded and stepped out at a small bar not far from his house. He'd never been here before, so he took in the area as he walked up.

He was led to a stool at the bar, explaining to the hostess that he was waiting on someone else. She had said she'd mark the seat next to him for her. Evan ordered a beer and settled in for a wait.

Two beers and half an hour later, she was late. He pulled out his phone and looked in the app to see if she had messaged him. It was empty since their dinner conversation where he hadn't replied other than to accept the date request.

He shrugged. If she wasn't coming, then it didn't really matter. He sent her a message instead.

E: *Sorry I missed you. Looks like it didn't work out again. I have to confess I only agreed to meet you to let you know, in person, that I wasn't going to continue our dates. We are both too busy right now and honestly, I fell for someone else. She may not have fallen for me yet, but I wanted to be honest with you tonight and explain.*

He hit send and picked up his third beer. It was already ordered and, once again, nothing had gone as planned, so he was going to make the best of it.

A few minutes later, the hostess returned to the seat next to him, and much to his complete surprise, Kayla slid onto the stool. A yellow sundress and a denim jacket greeted him with much more cheer than her fake smile.

"What are you doing here?" he asked. Not that he cared. He'd prefer to be sitting here with her over anyone else.

"You seem surprised to see me," she said.

Confused, Evan shook his head. "Well, yeah. I was supposed to be meeting someone else, but I'm so glad you're here instead."

Kayla ignored him and ordered a drink of her own. He stayed quiet until her drink was delivered, watching her and trying to figure out what was going on.

She took a sip of her mixed drink and looked at him over the rim of her glass. When she set it down, she gave him the saddest smile he'd ever seen on her.

"Hi, E." She held out her hand. "Nice to meet you. I'm K."

Chapter Twenty-Eight
Kayla

"You're K?" Evan choked out.

"One and the same," she told him.

In her head, this had gone differently. She was all anger and fire, but now that she was here, most of her fight was gone. She'd debated not even coming.

Emotions crossed Evan's face quickly before a smile settled in. "Of course it was you. That makes so much sense now."

"You aren't disappointed?" Kayla was the one to be shocked now.

"Hell, no. I've been trying to be something more with you since before this started, and you're telling me that we were kind of dating the whole time?"

Kayla hid behind another sip of her drink. Thousands of scenarios had played out in her mind about how tonight was going to go, and this wasn't one of them. Now she didn't know what to do.

"Seriously, Evan." She set her drink back down on the bar. "You were trying to sleep with me and continue this blind date nonsense. You're busted."

His jaw fell. "I came here to tell K in person that we weren't a match."

"Sure, now that you're caught red-handed you would say that." Kayla rolled her eyes at him.

"What? No!" He said a little too loudly and had other customers turning to look at them.

"Come on, Evan. You were all chatty last weekend and then called me. Then as soon as you got off the phone with me, you agreed to this date."

"First off, you set me up for this. Second, I messaged K because Cade encouraged me to do it and I had a few beers. I was upset over YOU and decided to see if I had any connection with the person in the app. I didn't. I made up my mind then to tell her I didn't want to date."

"You could have done that in the app, Evan."

"I could have," he agreed. "But I didn't want to. The person I spent a whole week talking to in that damn app deserved more than that. I didn't want to just disconnect without an explanation."

"Still could have done it in the app."

It didn't make sense. There was no reason for him to sit here and continue to lie to her. He was busted and yet still arguing.

"I couldn't explain it, though now it makes more sense, I needed to do it in person." Evan downed his beer and set it back on the bar.

She shook her head. He made her want to believe him, but she couldn't be in a relationship with someone she didn't trust.

"Think about it. We haven't talked since last week and even then it was nonsense."

He had her there, aside from one message that could be construed as flirty, the messages were bland. The conversation was nothing like it had been before she had slept with Evan as real her.

"I didn't even write you back again Friday. I only accepted the date," he continued. Then his eyes got big. "I did write you back! Check it."

"Evan, really, you have to give it up and just accept that you're caught." She sighed and debated just walking out.

"Please, Kayla. It's important."

She sighed again and pulled her phone out of her purse to look at it. She'd been running late to get here after debating if she was coming or not and hadn't looked at her phone since she left her house.

"Don't open it yet. Look at the time; that was before you got here," he pointed out.

"Okay," she agreed. It was sent about ten minutes before she showed up.

Kayla unlocked her phone and set it down on the bar so he could see it as she opened it. She quickly read the message and then read it again. He really had broken up with K. It didn't prove that had been his plan the whole time, but it was proof that he did.

"You could have made up your mind to do that after I was late and you thought I wasn't coming." She held on to that last small fraction of anger she still had.

He looked hurt and she wanted to take it back but still wasn't sure she trusted him. "I thought you knew me better than that. Talk to Cade then. I told him about it." All the fight was gone from him and she hated that she was the one to do that.

She blew out a breath. "Do you remember how I told you that I'd never had people that just did things for me and didn't ask for anything in return?"

He nodded. She was going to try to explain why she was so screwed up before he walked away.

"When I first met you, I told you I had owned a restaurant before. That's true, but I didn't leave to pursue other things like I said." She didn't tell this story ever, and it took her a minute to gather her thoughts to get it out. "I was in business with my ex-boyfriend. I wanted to open a restaurant, he'd offered to help back it, and everything was good."

"You don't have to tell me anything, Kayla." There was a bitter tone to his voice.

She'd screwed up, she knew that now. Something was telling her to believe him, but she'd pushed it down so deep that it was acrid as it rose up now, teasing her with the knowledge that she already had before she invented this mess.

"I do. Anyway, Kevin helped me launch the restaurant. It went well for a year. I ran everything, and he would make comments on the menu and staffing choices. All nonsense things really just to make him feel like an owner. One night I walked in on him in my office diddling the hostess. We weren't even closed, it was just that I wasn't supposed to be there."

"I'm sorry," Evan said.

She brushed it off, needing to tell him the rest. "I lost my cool, as you can imagine. He said he'd done all this for me with making the restaurant, and all I needed to do was be where I was supposed to and I wouldn't have known. In other words, it was my fault for showing up." She sighed. "I tried to get financing to buy the restaurant from him, but he wouldn't do it. I had put all the work in, and he kept it in exchange for me ruining his plans. I got a clean break from it. He hadn't put my name on anything, and I was too young and dumb to notice. It was all his and what he wanted was to be successful and not need to put in any real work."

Evan's fists had clenched on the bar. "What's his name?" he grunted out."

"Irrelevant, but I appreciate it. He's a jerk, but I'm better off. If I hadn't shown up when I did, I wouldn't have known and he would have kept doing it. I put everything I had into that restaurant, a full menu that I helped create. I used to cook there, too."

"That's why you insisted on the silent partner bit?" Evan asked.

She nodded. "It had nothing to do with you. It was just all my own fucked up feelings. It's also why I panicked when we slept together. I was so scared to get back into a situation where everything would be taken away from me."

"You could have just talked to me." Evan picked at the label on his beer.

"I should have. I was so scared, though. It's not an excuse, and I don't expect you to say anything. I just thought I would let you know.

For what it's worth, the blind date thing was never a test or anything of you. I kinda had a crush on you and just wanted to, I don't know, know what could have been?"

"Kayla," Evan said. He stood from the stool he was on and wrapped his arms around her. "I would never do anything like that to you. Ever. And the contract is good for the restaurant. I don't want to take it from you, couldn't do it."

"I know," she mumbled into his shirt. "I read that contract word for word and hired a lawyer to do the same."

"As you should have."

"I'm sorry I freaked out. I'm even more sorry that I accused you of being something that I know you're not." She sniffed, crying again. It was a wonder she had any tears left after all the crying she'd done this week.

"I'll give you the restaurant, free and clear. I told you before that I would."

Kayla pulled away so she could look up at him. "I don't want you to. I don't want you out of it. I just needed to remember who we were. I'm so sorry I crawled into my past and I couldn't find a way back out. I kept coming up with these scenarios and I freaked."

"Don't apologize for working through your own things. Just talk to me, please?"

She nodded. "I've missed you so much." Kayla grabbed a napkin off the bar and wiped at her face, cleaning up the tears as best as she could.

"What now?" Evan asked.

She tilted her head and pretended to ponder his question. Then she pressed her lips to his. Evan groaned and wrapped his arms around her again before pulling away.

"I missed you, too."

Chapter Twenty-Nine
Kayla

Last night, Kayla had made a decision. Evan was it for her. She wanted him and she was going to make it work with him. She still had some mess to work through in her brain, but she believed him

After she'd gone home, she'd realized it wasn't her gut that she'd been trusting—it was her fear. It had led her to do dumb things when it came to Evan, and she needed to stop.

He had forgiven her last night for acting a fool. They'd ended up getting a booth at the bar last night and had stayed for a while and eaten greasy food and talked. Then, hours later, they'd each gone home, alone. Well, almost; he'd dropped her off at home since she had taken a cab there, but nonetheless she went in alone.

Evan had texted her first thing this morning though. She had laid in bed and goofy smiled at it before she replied. One other realization she'd had last night was that she loved him. It had hit her in the face just before she'd bared all to him.

Now up and showered, she was a woman on a mission. She had on her sexiest lingerie, one of his button down shirts that he had left at her house, a pair of heels, and nothing else, save for a long coat she had on over it all. She was on her way to his house to surprise him.

Her nerves grew as she pulled up to his building. Butterflies danced around in her stomach as she parked, but her resolve held strong as she got out of the car. This was Evan, and he wanted her as much as she wanted him, that she knew.

She stood in front of his door, knocking twice, and waiting. When he didn't come down, she sighed and pulled out her phone to call him.

"Hey," he answered.

"Hey yourself. What are you doing?" she asked.

"Thinking about you."

"What a coincidence," she teased.

"What—are you thinking about me?" he asked.

"I'm thinking about showing up at your house in heels and sexy lingerie and one of your shirts," she said huskily.

"You should definitely put that plan into motion, Kayla," he said. "Or stay there, I can come to your place."

"Evan," she interrupted him moving around. "Come open the door for me, I'm not wearing much."

The phone fell. She heard the thunk of it connecting with something before he picked it back up. "I'm coming."

"I plan for you, too," she teased.

Evan yanked the door open and pulled her inside, slamming it shut behind them. She took a few steps in, her heels clicking on the hard floor. She spun to face him and untied the belt from her waist, letting the jacket fall open and off her shoulders.

"Kayla," Evan growled as he looked at her.

"Continue my fantasy, Evan. What would you do with me once I was here?"

He picked her up and tossed her over his shoulder. She laughed in surprise as one of his hands came up and swatted her butt lightly.

"I'd go caveman and put you in my bed."

She laughed, feeling happy for the first time in way too long.

Far more gentle than she expected him to be, Evan laid her on the bed. One by one he unbuttoned every button on his shirt, parting it like he was unwrapping a treasure as he did.

"You are everything," Evan said.

"You are my everything," she told him.

He looked down at her and backed away, standing up on the side of the bed. Her excitement grew. This was the same way that he had taken her before and she wanted it, needed it, again.

She watched as he undressed in front of her. Taking in every exposed inch of him as his gaze stayed on her. This man was perfection and he was all hers.

His muscles rippled as he moved, and she licked her lips in anticipation.

"Take it off," he demanded. "I swear if I touch it, I will rip it off of you."

She gasped, finding the idea way more exciting than she thought she would. Rising up, she slipped her arms out of his shirt and unclasped her bra. He watched her intently and she watched him. He was tense and she knew he was holding back.

"There," she said, laying back down and tossing her bra to the side.

"All of it," he growled.

She arched a brow at him, daring him to make good on his threat.

"Dammit, Kayla," he said. Reaching down, he tore the skimpy piece of fabric from her.

God, she loved it way more than she had any right to. Something like that shouldn't be as exciting as it was.

His hands roamed her body. She brought hers to his back, feeling his tensed muscles as he moved. What she wanted to feel was out of reach just yet, but she'd get there. She let her nails scratch him as she skated her hands back up to his neck.

"You're going to undo me before we get started," he said. "Put your hands up there."

He lifted her, turning her to put her head on the pillows and her hands at the headboard. She went willingly. She wanted to touch him, but the commanding way he was talking to her and taking charge was doing it for her right now.

He cupped both her breasts, pushing them up, again skating that line between too much and too little aggression, and it was just enough. She ached for him, silently willing him to move, touch her more, slide lower.

He reached down taking a nipple into his mouth, sucking hard and releasing before doing the same on the other. His hands squeezed her breasts up as he did.

"Please," she begged.

Evan almost gave her what she wanted as one hand slid lower, skating over what she needed most. "This?" he teased.

"Yes," she cried. If he didn't touch her, she was going to explode with need.

* * *

Exhausted, Kayla lay on Evan's bed staring at the ceiling above them.

"Penny for your thoughts?" Evan asked.

"I was just thinking about how I overthought all this and nearly missed my chance with you," Kayla answered honestly. It had been her own fault that things had taken as long as they did to get here.

"I wasn't going anywhere. I told you that, and I meant it. You're stuck with me." Evan pulled her closer to him.

"If only I had gotten past my own mess sooner. We could have been doing this for so much longer," she told him.

"Well, we just have to make up for lost time then," Evan smiled.

Kayla's stomach growled. She had gotten here late in the morning, and it was already dark outside. All they had done was burn calories so at some point she needed to eat.

"After I feed you," he teased her. "Get up. Let's go see what I can make you."

"Or, we can order delivery from here and come up with some

other way to pass the time." She smirked at him.

"I like the way you think," he said. "Where is my phone?"

Kayla laughed as Evan stood up looking for his phone. She hadn't seen it, or hers for that matter, since she'd gotten here.

"Damn," he said as he picked it up. "Jake's been calling me."

Kayla wrapped the sheet around her and got up as well. "My phone is definitely downstairs."

"Stay. I'll go get it."

Evan left the room already dialing Jake. She took the time to straighten the blankets that they had made a mess of and grabbed Evan's shirt and put it back on.

He walked back into the room still on the phone and handed her purse to her. "I'm going to put you on speaker with Kayla," he said and then set the phone down. "Okay go ahead."

"I've tried calling both of you to let you know that the last lead panned out. We were able to verify that it was her and then contact the police. I told them about the blackmail too, which has been pretty public, but I wanted to let you know in case they call you. My guys are still watching to make sure she doesn't leave, and the police have said they will pick her up today." Jake blew out a breath. "I'll feel better when they have her."

"That's great," Kayla told him.

"Really, man. Thanks a lot for your help with this," Evan said.

"It's the least I could do," Jake said. "Kayla, I tried calling you and so did Lauren. I'll let her know that you're, umm, occupied."

Kayla laughed.

"Hey, thanks for the blind date pick. I got there on my own, though." Evan pulled her close to him.

"Doesn't matter how you got there, I'm just glad you did."

"Later, man. I'll call you tomorrow."

"I'll send a text when they pick her up," Jake said.

Jake ended the call and Evan looked down at her. "I'm so glad that's getting resolved."

"Me, too."

Chapter Thirty
Evan

Evan had taken Kayla home Monday morning to shower and get ready. They were due at Catherine's for a meeting with police, lawyers, and Thomas. Apparently, there were some unanswered questions, and the police needed the proof of the blackmail attempts.

"Ready!" Kayla came out of her bedroom dressed for the day, hair and make-up completely done.

"You know I'm just going to mess that all up later, right?" he joked as he got closer to her.

"Promises, promises," she teased back.

"Let's go get this done."

They headed out and were quickly at Catherine's office. Their plan had been to meet with her about a half hour before to discuss what was going on and to get everything ready.

"I'm so happy for you guys!" Catherine squealed as they walked in holding hands.

"Thank you," Kayla said and gave her friend a one-armed hug.

They followed her back to the conference room. "I took the

liberty of printing out all of the emails, and Thomas, who will be here shortly, printed out whatever technical information he has. With any luck this will be over very soon. Is your lawyer on her way?" Catherine asked Evan.

"She is. I emailed her what we knew, but I don't know if it even made sense."

Probably because Kayla had been up with him for damn near 24 hours before they sent that email. "She's going to be cutting it close time-wise though," Evan added.

"No problem. The front desk knows who to expect."

They talked about a few other things, and Catherine circled back to their new couple status several times. She was genuinely happy for them, and it was a bit overwhelming but in a good way for him.

"Thomas," Catherine greeted the newcomer. "Thank you for coming, and for all your help. This is Kayla and Evan." She did the introductions and they took their seats as they waited for everyone to come.

Over the next ten minutes, the room filled with different detectives. Cade was also there; he was too nosy to be in the same building and not come down, and April, Kayla's lawyer, arrived too.

"I think that's everyone," Kayla told the lead detective.

"Great," the lead detective who had introduced himself as Detective Lawson said.

Over the next two hours, the room was filled and everyone talked over what they knew as the police asked questions. Thomas had been very detailed, but Evan still had no idea what he was talking about. Well, he had an idea, but looking at it made no sense to him.

"Thank you, everyone," Detective Lawson said. "I have a question and would like to get the insight of those who were impacted. After meeting with the subject and now after reading all these emails, do you think she sent them?"

Damn, Evan thought, that meant they were right and they hadn't come from her. "I don't think so."

"Me either," Cade said. "The language used is too inconsistent from the person to the email. It almost seems like their goal wasn't to get money."

Detective Lawson nodded his agreement. "Anyone else?"

Evan added, "It's been something we were wondering about, but we don't have any suspects that would be working with her."

"You could definitely ask her daughter. I could call her and have her here shortly," Kayla offered.

"I will speak to them separately due to the sensitive nature of her involvement."

Evan suppressed a snort. Lauren wasn't involved. She didn't like her mother and there was plenty of proof of their most recent falling out, which had overlapped with a different smear campaign on the restaurant as it was.

Catherine added Evan's thoughts. "I included here in the files I emailed over and in the printouts in your packets the information of the last run-in with her. Please, let any of us know if we missed anything and, of course, you can ask Lauren directly."

"I appreciate it," Detective Lawson told her. "If you ever want to do something else, you are welcome to run every briefing at the department. This has been the most well-planned interview I've done with witnesses, with evidence and everything ready to go for me already."

Evan watched as Catherine blushed. She was overly happy most of the time, but in the years he'd known her, he had never seen her blush.

"Thank you. I'll keep that in mind," she said.

"We will see ourselves out." He stood and shook everyone's hands. "Thomas, we might be in touch with questions, but thank you for your help. If anyone thinks of someone she could have been working with, please let us know. We will question her about it, but I'm not sure we will get much information. She's been quiet."

They left the room and Catherine finally took a seat. "I'm using this mess in my portfolio. None of you made me sign an NDA."

Kayla laughed. "I will sign a release if you want. By all means, use whatever April says is okay."

"The only thing I would caution is how soon you use it. Technically, this is an ongoing investigation," April said.

Evan had met April a few times, but those were few and far between. Overall most of the legal work for Blind Date when Evan came in had been done by his own lawyers and she'd only reviewed it with Kayla.

She was shorter than everyone here, just over 5 foot if he had to guess. She had long dark brown hair that hung to her waist and carried a bag with her that he was pretty sure would tip her over if it became off-balance.

"Understood on that front. I really mean the circumstances, not so much this part," Catherine gestured to the room.

"I've had a lot of apology emails come through. Some people are still angry and want to be removed from the system, but I'm pretty sure things are going to be okay for the restaurant," Kayla told them.

Evan dropped a kiss on her head as he stood, walking around the table to Cade. "Thanks for coming, man."

"You know I wouldn't miss it. I do have to get back to work, though." Quickly, Cade left.

Evan arched an eyebrow at Catherine who shrugged. That wasn't entirely out of character for him, but it seemed to come out of nowhere.

"I'm glad it's mostly over now though," Evan said.

"We've still got a bit to go before it's done, but at least they have her locked up for now," April said. "Catherine, can I talk to you?"

"Sure." Catherine walked April out after she said her goodbyes.

"Thank you," Kayla said.

Evan went to her and brought her in for a hug. "For what?" he asked.

"For being you."

He leaned down and kissed her. "Thank you for being you, too."

· · ·

Evan

Thank you for reading! I hope you enjoyed Kayla and Evan's story and if you did, keep reading to get Owen's story for free and learn about the other books in the Billionaire Blind Dates series!

Keep in touch with Toni Denise

Follow Toni Denise on Social Media!
Facebook
Instagram
Twitter
And Sign up for her Newsletter to find out about awesome games
and new releases.
Sign up here!

Owen

Don't miss the prequel novella, Owen's story.

Owen is a man who always knows and gets what he wants, but when he goes to the bar to grab a nightcap, he gets more than he bargained for. He meets a woman who's unlike any he's ever known but saying goodbye to bachelorhood will take some convincing.

Jenna isn't thrilled with the idea of going on a blind date, but a deal is a deal, so she shows up. She meets a great guy, who saves her from what would've been a disastrous date. Unfortunately, she never hears from him again.

Even though, the unplanned date goes well, Owen has a big decision to make. Is Jenna the one who will make him rethink bachelorhood?

Find out what happens in the prequel novella to the Billionaire Blind Date Series!

To read the full story, sign up for my newsletter!
www.tonidenisebooks.com

Owen Chapter 1

Owen stepped into The Striped Keg bar and looked around. The dim lighting was a stark contrast to the well-lit street he had just come in from.

Men and women chatted throughout the room, most standing at tables with a few lining the bar. He came here specifically to avoid too much conversation. Plus, as it was across town, no one recognized him.

They could if they looked hard enough, but few ever did, and that was what he wanted. A drink and some peace.

Walking around the old wooden bar, he took a seat at the far end and waited for the bartender to notice him. It had been a disastrous week, one he'd like to forget, and here where he blended in, it helped.

"What can I get ya?" the bartender asked.

He handed over his card. "Start a tab. I have a ride home, didn't drive here. Scotch."

He always made it a point to let the bartender know he wasn't driving. It helped make sure he wasn't cut off before he was done for the night.

"All right." With a curt nod the bartender walked away.

"Excuse me?" A pretty blonde in a black dress approached him. "Are you Kyle?"

Owen shook his head.

"Damn. Mind if I sit here?" she asked as she set her small purse on the bar and sat down without waiting for an answer. "Why I let my sister set me up on some stupid blind date with a guy name Kyle of all things, I'll never know. Then he's not even here on time? Way to set the tone."

As much as he didn't want to be, he had to admit he was intrigued by the plain-speaking woman next to him. She didn't even seem to care if anyone was listening to her monologue, just kept on going.

The bartender brought Owen's drink over and turned to the woman.

"A beer, please. Whatever's on tap is fine."

"Add it to my tab," Owen said without thinking.

It was stupid. She was going to sit here now and keep talking to him and there went all hope for his night of peace.

"You don't have to do that," she told him as the bartender walked away.

"Looks like you could use a good break tonight, figured maybe it would cheer you up."

"I'm not going to sleep with you," she said boldly, causing Owen to choke on his first sip.

"What?"

"Just because you bought me a drink and my date didn't show, I'm not so grateful that I'll drop my panties for you tonight. I don't do one-night stands."

Owen couldn't hold back the bark of laughter that spilled out. "You're very blunt," he told her.

"No sense in not saying what you mean here in a dark bar with strangers. If you want, I can pay for my drink myself when he comes back with it."

"It's okay. I don't mind paying for it with nothing in return." He flashed his most charming smile at her. "I didn't intend to get anything for it as it was."

"Thank you."

Her drink showed up a moment later and he let the bartender know she was on his tab until he closed out.

"Why'd you think I was your date?"

"Wishful thinking, perhaps?" She shook her head at herself before turning back to him. "You were late getting here and your tie is the right color."

"My tie?" It was a light green, one he wore often, favoring the color.

"Yeah, he's supposed to be wearing a green tie. That's vague enough, but what shade of green? There's so many, and then so many men in here with green ties."

He nodded as he listened to her ramble on about ties. She was animated when she talked, and he found himself enjoying it and her company. Normally he carried the conversations but didn't feel the need to with her.

"Sorry," she said suddenly.

"For what?" He tilted his head, trying to figure out what happened.

"I always talk too much. It's a fault of mine and annoys people." She sipped her beer as though that was making it all better because she couldn't talk.

"Oddly enough, I was enjoying your speech on ties and the various colors of green."

"Liar," she said but then grinned up at him.

"I am in a position where I don't want to be the only one talking but I seem to always be doing just that. Having someone I don't need to pretend I want to do all the talking with is refreshing."

"Well, flattery will get you everywhere," she laughed. "Except my bed."

"Got it. Not sleeping together tonight."

She shook her head but laughed.

"Excuse me, are you Jenna?" A man in a poor-fitting suit stood next to her.

Still facing him, he could see the indecision on her face as she looked back at who had to be Kyle. He looked like a jerk and was definitely older than both of them.

Finally, she answered, "I am. Are you Kyle?"

He nodded and then didn't even bother to hide it as he checked her out from head to toe. "Must be my lucky night. You are stunning."

Owen rolled his eyes and sipped his scotch. This guy was going to get nowhere with her and he was interested in watching it happen.

"Sorry, if you were looking for a hookup, let me save you the time. I won't be sleeping with you for at least a few months, if you last that long."

Thank God he had already swallowed his drink or he would have choked on it again. Owen let a small smile sneak out as he watched Kyle try to decide what to say to that.

"Months?" Kyle asked, the shock evident on his face.

"At least three, maybe six," Jenna confirmed.

"Umm, well, I," Kyle stammered and pulled at his collar.

Taking pity on him, Owen jumped into the conversation. "Dude, just cut your losses and find a new bar and date."

Kyle seemed to just register his presence as his gaze slid to Owen. "I mean, it's not that we had to tonight, but like, that's a long time."

Owen just shook his head. "Go on."

Kyle seemed slightly relieved as he spun and disappeared into the crowded bar.

"You really should have let him sweat it out a bit longer."

"Couldn't. The man looked like he was going to pop before he ever managed a sentence."

"A pity he was only looking to get laid. I'm never letting my sister set me up again. Where'd she even meet him?"

Owen laughed. "He looks like a used car salesman, and not a very good one."

Jenna threw her head back and laughed. "God, yes. That's exactly it."

"Months, huh?' Owen arched an eyebrow at her.

"For him? Absolutely. If ever." She looked at her phone. "He's almost an hour late and was clearly checking me out before he decided if he wanted to have the date. It's going to be a no, bud."

"Bud?" Owen teased.

"He looks like he calls people bud."

He agreed and nodded. The man one hundred percent looked like he did. "Well, now that you have no date tonight, what are you going to do?"

"You're not my date?" Jenna fake pouted before giggling. "Don't look so horrified. I'm not trying to trap you."

"Not horrified, more curious," he answered simply. "So what was supposed to happen on this date?" Curious now, he found he wanted to keep the conversation going and know more about her.

"I assumed we'd chat over drinks and decide if we wanted a second date. Didn't really think about it that deep to be honest."

"What a crummy date," Owen said.

"I agree. I really should have just stayed home."

"Now, that I wouldn't have agreed with."

Just then Kyle walked by again. "Months," he muttered, shaking his head before turning into the crowd again.

"Dude's a creep," Owen observed. "Want to get out of here?" he asked her.

Jenna pinned him with a look that had him backpedaling.

"To get pizza. I swear. It's walking distance, too."

She stared at him for a moment, and he knew she was deciding whether to believe him or not before she nodded.

"Bartender!" Owen called. "I think we're ready to pay." So much for the tab he'd been planning to run up.

Liked it? Get it for free by signing up for my newsletter at www.tonidenisebooks.com

Cade

Coming up next...

Cade has a secret. One that could destroy his friendships and wreck his business, and it's all his father's fault.

Everything that Cade has worked for has been under the pressure of his father breathing down his neck until recently. Completely fed up with the pressure and not being able to run the company the way he wants, he parted ways with his father. That led to threats from his father and then actions against his friends.

April has worked herself to the bone to reach her dream of becoming a partner at her law firm. Now, with that just in reach, she isn't sure it's what she wants and someone is trying to take it all from her.

When a misguided attempt to set them up goes wrong, April is forced to confront the feelings that she had for Cade may never have gone. Cade offers her a contract marriage in exchange for his help to get her career back on track, all she has to do is play the perfect wife everywhere but the bedroom.

Cade

What happens when a secret too big to keep comes to light and April ends up in the crossfire? Will Cade risk it all to save her?

Also by Toni Denise

Learn More or get buy links for any of these books at my author website:

tonidenisebooks.com

Westbeach Series:

Old Friends

On the Run

One Last Chance

Out of Time

Series Boxset

Finding Love Series:

Engaged to Her Neighbor

Married to the Playboy

Falling for Her Fake Husband

Short and Steamy Duet:

The Wedding Date

The Wedding Ruse

Stone Twins Duet:

Please Stay

Don't Leave

(Don't Leave is included in the "Mine This Winter" collection available Dec 1, 2022)

Bonus Content Old Friends

Sometimes a second chance can be the last chance.

Recently divorced, Kelly finds herself back in her hometown. Deciding that starting over is key, she and her son take to living a new life.

When a second chance with Mason, an old flame, ignites, Kelly is excited to feel love again.

But something is wrong. Someone is watching them, waiting to strike. Someone that knows them. Someone. . . close.

Not knowing who she can trust, Kelly is thrust into a life of fear and looking over her shoulder.

Where do you turn when the one person you thought you could trust might actually be the person you're running from?

A steamy romance novel with a moderate heat level.

Old Friends Chapter 1

Taking in the scenery, Kelly wondered why she never came back to visit. Going home was hard, but it was only about a four-hour drive. She really should have come home before now. Taking the long road around the outside of town, the scenery alternated between trees so dense the automatic headlights came on in her car and open pastures with cows or horses in them. This time of year, everything was still bright green. It looked pretty, but she knew better; being late August, it was hot out there. Soon the brilliant green would give way to a wonder of colors as fall slowly crept in.

Turning the music down, she focused on the GPS and the last few miles of her trip. Traffic had started to pick up in the previous hour of her journey until she left the interstate. She was glad she had left earlier in the day; it was only about 4:00 p.m. now. A quick check of the back seat showed Hunter was waking up. For a seven-year-old, he wasn't a bad road-trip partner, but he had slept all but the first hour, when he ate most of the snacks. "Hey, Hunt, we're almost there. Are you excited?"

"Are we in a zoo?" Hunter sleepily asked.

Kelly took another look around, wondering why this was even a question. Cows. There were cows on both sides of the road. "No, baby, there are ranches around here that raise cows."

"So, I'll see the zoo every day?"

"Yes." Simpler to agree than to explain more as he wasn't awake yet. Besides, in all his seven years, he'd never seen the countryside, and Westbeach was about as opposite of DC as you could get.

As they made the last turn, the woods on either side were a welcome presence, adding shade to the last bit of the trip, which had been mostly on the sunny highway. She was going to have a sunglasses tan for sure. Finally pulling in to the driveway, Kelly breathed a sigh of relief to see her aunt and uncle already there and waiting for them.

The light blue house was one level and had a small new porch on the front. The wood was still white looking, so she could tell it hadn't been there long. The front yard was freshly cut, and there were trees on both sides of the property and behind it. A privacy fence, which also looked new, wrapped around the backyard. No neighbors could be seen unless you were in the road. *Wonder if I'll be able to sleep without the noise of the city?*

Aunt Mary was the first to come off the porch as Kelly parked the car. Mary, in her signature flower dress and floppy hat over her white hair, had always been able to style anything except herself. Her dresses were like something older ladies probably wore in the fifties. Gardening, cooking, shopping—same dresses; some things never changed. Bob, on the other hand, was a jeans and T-shirt man. Kelly could never remember Uncle Bob having hair—on his head or face. Much like Mary though, his style was the same no matter what he was doing. The only thing these two changed was the colors each day.

When Kelly stepped out of her car, Aunt Mary immediately wrapped her in a welcoming hug. "How are you doin', dear? How was the trip?"

"Let her get out of the car, Mary." Uncle Bob always sounded a tad sour but was a sweetheart underneath.

"I am, I am." Aunt Mary backed up and opened the back door for Hunter to climb out of the car. "Hunter! You've gotten so big!" Hunter grinned and stood tall at her praise. Mary ruffled his hair and proceeded to go to the trunk with Uncle Bob to get their bags. "Is this all you brought, honey?"

"For now. The rest is packed, and Dylan is supposed to send it this week, but we'll see if he remembers to let the movers in or not."

"Okay, let us know if you forgot anything." Aunt Mary smiled sadly at Kelly.

"You know I will." She plastered on a big smile to reassure everyone that she really was okay. Taking Hunter's hand, she turned and walked into the house.

When she walked in, the first thing she noticed was that the house was fully furnished; some things even looked new. A gray sofa in the living room faced a flat-screen TV with a small coffee table. Passing through the living room to the kitchen, she noticed there was a cherry-colored table for four with a bouquet of fresh flowers waiting for them. *Definitely Aunt Mary's idea.* And the smell—some version of every spice, but in a good way—was just like Bob and Mary's house. It was a welcoming scent, the smell of home.

Kelly walked down the hall of the modest one-story house, pulling her suitcase behind her. Three rooms, two bathrooms—per Mary's directions, hers was the last on the left. The room had a large queen-sized bed in the center with a gorgeous purple quilt and matching pillows on it. A dresser sat against the long wall with a mirror attached.

Checking all the doors, she discovered the closet was behind the open bedroom door, and against the wall was a master bath. A purple shower curtain hung already with silver bath mats. Aunt Mary really should have been an interior designer, and her remembering Kelly's favorite color just made it that much better.

Kelly had never been able to have everything decorated in her favorite color before, but now she could do her thing. Putting her bag down she took a deep breath; divorce wasn't going to be too bad if this was how it started. Coming back home wasn't all that bad, even if it did make her feel a little like a failure for her marriage not working.

There was no love lost in her marriage anyway. Dylan didn't even fight for custody of Hunter. He just let them go and agreed to everything—not that she had asked for much, just child support and custody. Dylan didn't even want weekends with Hunter. Kelly sighed as she looked in the mirror and pulled her hair into a ponytail before heading back out to the other three noisily chatting about cows in the dining room.

"Hunter tells me he's excited to see the zoo every day," Uncle Bob informed her with a laugh as he pulled Kelly up for a quick hug. Although pushing seventy, Bob was still a tall man. He was the exact opposite of Mary, who was shorter than Kelly by five inches, standing at five feet tall. The family had always joked that it was her hat that gave her an inch or two and that she genuinely was less than five feet. Mary had always laughed along as well, shushing everyone, but never argued it.

"Something tells me he'll eventually tire of it," Kelly said with a small laugh of her own.

"I stocked some essentials in the cabinets and fridge; wasn't sure what all you would need. We can go to dinner later, or you can come over and I'll cook." Aunt Mary always made sure everyone had eaten. If you weren't hungry, she was going to have you doing something until you were. "We are waiting on the handyman though. The disposal isn't working right now."

"No problem, and we can eat whatever is easiest for you tonight. Thank you guys again." Bending down, she hugged Aunt Mary again and gave her a kiss on the cheek. "I don't know what I would do without you guys here."

"Family helps family, dear." And that was all Aunt Mary was going to say about it. No thanks needed ever.

"I love you." Before either of them did more than tear up, Kelly changed the subject. "The handyman? Is that who redid the front porch? It looks nice."

"Yes, yes. Bob thought he was going to do it. Took the boards off and then decided it was too much for one old man, like I said." She cut a look at Bob, who decided not to say anything and continued to talk to Hunter. "Thankfully," Mary continued, "the handyman was able to get out here and get it done before you got here."

"Really?" Hunter shouted and jumped up from the table to run out the back door.

"I told him there was a swing set out there." Bob smiled and moved to follow Hunter out the door.

"He will never come inside again." Kelly laughed and moved to the window to see Hunter happily swinging while Uncle Bob looked on.

"Go unpack, and I'll wait right here for the doorbell," Mary said while shooing Kelly from the window. "He'll be fine."

"I know. I'll be in his room for now if you need me."

Wandering down the hall, Kelly opened the door across from her room and was pleased to find an office. Mary really had thought of everything. A small desk sat facing the window with a fancy-looking high-backed office chair, and she could see the entire backyard from there. A tall lamp in the corner would keep her from having to turn on the overhead light to see, and a ceiling fan was a nice addition. The room was painted a darker shade of blue, but it didn't seem to make the room feel smaller.

There was plenty of room left in there for her treadmill since there was no gym here that she knew of, and going for a run would be difficult with Hunter still home for the summer. Mary always knew what worked and what didn't without even trying. Kelly would be glad to get back to work in two weeks in her new office. Thankfully, her legal transcription was work from home, and they had been generous with her time off under the circumstances. She would have a pile of work when she got back to it though. It was going to be rough going back to work after all this time off. Thinking about her emails that she hadn't checked all day, she walked out of the room and closed the door.

Moving on, Kelly checked the room next to hers and saw a twin bed, some toys already set out for Hunter, and a large baseball poster on the wall across from her. Smiling, she walked over and touched it, amazed by the little things Bob and Mary had thought of to help Hunter adjust. She'd also bet money that there was no swing set here before Kelly decided to move in. Kelly heaved Hunter's suitcase on the bed and started to unpack and put away the clothes.

"I didn't pack hangers." Kelly let out a deep sigh. "If this is the worst part, I'm good, right?" Musing to herself, she walked down the hall to see if Mary wanted to go to the store. "Mary, are you interested in running to the—" Seeing a man in the kitchen, Kelly stopped midsentence.

"Kelly, this is Mason, the handyman. Mason, do you remember Kelly?"

"How could I forget?" Drying his hands off, he looked up, and Kelly stared into eyes she hadn't seen in twelve years. Mason Cole.

"Wow! How are you? It's been forever." Not sure what to do with herself, she leaned awkwardly against the wall, taking in this man who had been a teenager when she saw him last. Instead, here was this man with his dark brown hair and muscles she could see through his blue shirt. And those blue eyes... a woman could get lost in those eyes. He hadn't changed much other than getting older, like her she supposed. He was still as handsome as ever.

"How's the set working out?" Mason interrupted Kelly's assessment of him. Oh, that smile, crooked with one dimple on the right cheek. That smile could make women fall all over themselves to get a glimpse of it. Nope, that hadn't changed one bit.

"Hunter is already out there." Mary saved her from having to form an answer. Nothing could have prepared Kelly for seeing this man in her kitchen.

Swallowing down old feelings and trying to move forward, Kelly shifted to look out the window on the back door to see Hunter still outside playing. Taking it in for the first time, she noticed the back deck was only slightly above ground level, just one step up. *I need to get a table and chairs for out here, so I can work and watch Hunter play.* The yard was a fair size, plenty of room for Hunter to run around, and the start of the tree line had been fenced into the yard, giving him a shaded place to play. The swing set was a good size as well, containing two swings, a slide, and monkey bars on one end. Uncle Bob strolled from the deck to the yard, watching Hunter wear himself out. *At least he'll sleep tonight, even after that long nap in the car.*

"What did you need, dear?" Aunt Mary asked.

"Oh, I didn't pack hangers and was wondering where the closest store was?" She focused on Mary, anything to not stare at this too-hot-to-be-here man in the kitchen.

"That would still be Gersham's down on Main Street. I have to head there to order the part for your disposal if you'd like a ride?" Of course, it was Mason who answered. And a ride, really? Lord knew she wanted to go for a ride. Wait, where had that thought come from? How unlike her; must be the nerves.

"I don't want to impose. I can head down there later."

"No imposing at all. Grab your bag and hop in the truck." Interesting how the words he chose said he made the decision, but the tone made it clear it was still her call.

Grabbing her bag, she let Hunter know she would be right back. For all he cared though, he was still enthralled with the swings and slide out back. After hugging Aunt Mary, she walked out to the dark blue Dodge Ram sitting in her driveway. Mason was standing by the truck and opened the door for her. He waited until she had settled before closing it. *What am I supposed to say now? What do I do?* Placing her bag in her lap, she sat still as he climbed in and backed out the driveway. Not much was said on the way to the store.

Staring out the passenger window, she watched the scenery. Everything seemed the same, and yet it all seemed so different at the same time. When they got to the store, they went their separate ways after Mason pointed her in the right direction. She grabbed several packs of hangers and headed toward the checkout. Mason was already standing there putting in an order for whatever part it was he needed.

As she approached, a shiver ran down her spine. Kelly felt like someone was watching her. Looking around, she didn't see anyone else in the store besides Mason and the clerk. Still, she picked up her pace, unable to shake the creepy feeling. She set the hangers on the counter, continuing to look around while waiting for them to finish. *You're losing it. No one is in here, just the empty store getting you creeped out.*

Needing a distraction, she watched the interaction going on at the register. The woman was practically hanging on Mason's every word like she was super interested in garbage disposals. Kelly rolled her eyes. When she looked up again, Mason winked at her. She had been caught. Completely distracted from the creepy feeling, she now had a new one—full-on embarrassment.

Part ordered and hangers paid for, they walked back to the truck again. Mason took the awkward bags of hangers and opened her door for her. While Kelly buckled in, he put the bags in the back seat, then shut her door and got in.

"Didn't like her much, did you?"

Kelly felt the heat creep up her face. He wasn't going to ignore her eye roll. "It wasn't that. More of a disbelief type of thing." *There, that makes me sound less rude for not liking someone I don't even know and positively not jealous.*

"Nope, it's been a while, but you still can't hide anything. It's all over your face," he teased.

Kelly put her hand to her heart and leaned toward Mason, doing an exaggerated impersonation of the busty clerk. "Oh, please tell me more about garbage disposals." She batted her lashes. "I just don't know what I would do without you having come in today, Mason." Kelly laughed and sat back right in the seat.

"Pretty good impression actually. Now you know why I didn't want to go to the store alone." Mason cut her a sly look but laughed as well. After a moment, they both fell into a companionable silence for the rest of the trip. Pulling up, Mason stopped her from opening the door with a hand on her shoulder. "It's good to see you and have you home again, even if it's not under the best of circumstances."

"Thank you. I'm glad to be home. No love lost in the reason for my coming home, so no worries. I'm glad I got to see you."

"If you need anything while you're here, let me give you my number. Your aunt and uncle call when something needs to be done in one of their rentals. Most of your new home has been newly renovated though; they really went all out to make it right for you. Oh, and I'll let Bob know when the part comes in. She said Tuesday, but when I pick it up will depend on when I can get someone to go to the store with me." Mason laughed again.

"I noticed. The porch looks great, and the swing set too. If you let me know when the part is ready, I can run in and pick it up, and then you can avoid the store altogether." Kelly winked at him. "You can just let me know. Let me find a paper, and I'll give you my number." She dug through her bag and came up with a crayon and a receipt. Blushing again at how much of a mess she must seem, she wrote her number down and handed it to him. Saying their goodbyes, she hopped out of the truck and went inside with a smile on her face.

\#

Kelly Marie Holstead, he didn't know she would be there today. He could have sworn it was tomorrow that Mary said she would get here. Pulling into his own driveway, he smiled as he remembered Kelly's reaction to Darlene, the clerk at Gersham's. Just like the old Kelly would have done, she let loose with that cute little eye roll. Heading inside, he greeted Shep, his aging yellow lab, with a pat on the head. Shep followed him through the house, waiting to be let outside. Grabbing a beer from the fridge, Mason opened the back door and went out to the deck, Shep in tow.

Checking his phone, he texted Nate, his brother and business partner, about the disposal and the part needed. He pulled Kelly's crayon-written number out of his pocket and plugged it into his phone. *Should I text her now, so she has my number? Is it too soon?*

After deciding to just program the number in and debate it later, his thoughts wandered to the day he had. After a rough morning with two young guys late to work, again, he was frustrated and cranky when he remembered he was supposed to check on Kelly's disposal today. When he pulled up, he was in no mood for small talk with Mary but had resigned himself to it. Then he noticed another car in the driveway.

Kelly apparently hadn't been expecting him. He wasn't entirely expecting her either. He hadn't seen her in almost twelve years, since they were seventeen and about to graduate high school. That summer was some of the best memories he had though. Kelly was his best friend, but when they went to college in different states, they had slowly lost touch. It was one of his biggest regrets. He and Kelly had shared everything—sometimes too much, but he could always tell her anything, and she, him. He knew Kelly had gotten married right after she graduated college, and that was about it.

She still looked as good as ever, a more mature woman and no longer the body of a teenager, but time had been kind to her. Her blonde hair had been pulled back, but it was more than shoulder length and had some highlights. Her body though, she looked like she took care of herself; he could see her defined leg muscles under her shorts. Her curves were more significant than he remembered. She wore no makeup, probably not something she usually did, but no reason to get dolled up for a road trip to move. He liked the no makeup look though, no pretending, nothing to hide.

Just then his phone went off, pulling him out of his thoughts as they headed in the wrong direction. Texting Nate back, he got up, adjusted his pants, and Shep followed him in the door. Nate was going to give him a hard time about seeing Kelly, and about venturing into Gersham's when he knew Darlene would be working. He wasn't kidding; he had taken Kelly as a bit of a buffer. Darlene always shamelessly threw herself at him, but she'd limit it to flirting if there was someone else in the store. The woman never took the hint that he wasn't interested, even though he had tried to let her down gently many times before. Now he just avoided the place when he knew she was working.

Time to make dinner. Pulling out the chicken, he got started on cooking. *Wonder if she still cooks as well as she used to?* What the hell was he doing, thinking about her so much? It had only been a few minutes, and nothing had even happened to make him feel so much about her. She hadn't thrown herself at him like most women, so what was it?

Finishing up dinner, he carried it to the living room. Watching TV would distract his wayward thoughts.

\#

He waited in his car with the lights off until Mason had finally left Kelly's house. He had watched her from the back of the store as she searched hangers. He couldn't believe she had been home just a few hours and was already back with Mason. How had that happened? Had to be her meddling aunt. He had been watching the house for the past week waiting for her arrival and would meet her again soon. She was supposed to come back after she finished school, and like a fool, he had expected her to, but no, she went and got married and hadn't come back at all.

He had followed her online for a long time and had made sure she found out about her husband's cheating. Chuckling to himself, he remembered how easy that had been. He had just pretended to be the secretary's doctor and called their house phone looking for the father of the baby. Of course, Kelly had answered. Then he "accidentally" spilled the news of the baby to her. He had gotten her home now. She hadn't been happy in her marriage anyway, so he didn't feel bad. This time, she would be his, and neither Mason nor anything else was going to stand in his way. He carefully put away his phone, excited to have new photos of her on it, and headed home.